CHEYENNE CAPTIVES

LEWIS B. PATTEN

SAGEBRUSH
Large Print Westerns

First published in Great Britain by Hale
First published in the United States by Doubleday

First Isis Edition
published 2020
by arrangement with
Golden West Literary Agency

A catalogue record for this book is available
from the British Library.

ISBN 978-1-78541-851-8

Published by
Ulverscroft Limited
Anstey, Leicestershire

Set by Words & Graphics Ltd.
Anstey, Leicestershire
Printed and bound in Great Britain by
T. J. International Ltd., Padstow, Cornwall

This book is printed on acid-free paper

CHAPTER
ONE

Julia Holley, taking clothes from the line stretched between the corner of the back porch and a young cottonwood in the center of the yard, paused for an instant, her left arm piled high with dry clothing. Clothespins filled the pockets of the apron tied around her waist.

She lifted her glance and stared out at the rolling southern Kansas landscape, wondering what had drawn her attention. It looked the same as it had on a thousand other Indian summer days. Tall dry grass waved in the slight afternoon breeze. The shallow draw running from north to south and passing through one corner of the corral, supplying a trickle of water for the three horses inside, looked exactly as it always had. Over her head, the windmill turned briskly, creaking with each stroke of the pump.

Her eyes picked up a small flock of birds and instantly she knew it was the birds that had drawn her glance. Something out there in the high grass had made them fly.

The movements of her hands became automatic. Her attention still seemed to be on what she was doing, but now there was a feeling of numbing cold running along her spine. There was a sharp tightening in her chest. Maybe a skulking coyote had spooked the birds. But maybe it had been something else. It didn't pay to assume anything.

Suddenly she noticed the horses in the corral. Instead of standing, heads down, idly switching at flies with their tails, they had grouped attentively at the side of the corral. All were staring toward something they had either seen or smelled south along the draw in the direction from which the birds had risen only a few moments earlier.

The coldness in Julia's spine and the tightening in her chest were recognizable as panic now. She wanted to drop the clothes and run but she did not. She continued taking clothing off the line, the only difference being that she hurried more.

She knew what was out there in the high grass and the knowledge filled her with raw terror. Biting her lip, she finished and walked toward the house, taking care neither to hurry nor to look around.

Inside, she slammed the door and dropped the stout bar into place. Sally Denton, her closest neighbor, who was staying with her while both their husbands were gathering cattle for shipment from Dodge City, was at the ironing board beside the stove, ironing some of young Frankie Denton's overalls. Sally glanced up, failed to see the terror in Julia's eyes, and glanced quickly back to her work.

Julia dumped the clean, dry clothes on the kitchen table. She went first to the window that faced toward the corral.

The horses were getting nervous now, fidgeting, raising their heads to sniff the breeze, stamping their feet and snorting occasionally.

Julia closed the window and fastened it. She closed the heavy wooden shutters and bolted them, top and bottom.

Sally glanced up at her with mild puzzlement, for the day was warm. "Leave it open," she said. "It's so beautiful out today."

Julia shook a warning head at her and put a finger to her lips. She shot a glance at three-year-old Frankie, playing with some homemade wooden toys on the floor. She went on to the next window, closing it similarly and bolting the shutters over it.

Sally, her own face pale now, started to say something, then closed her mouth and licked her colorless lips. She put the iron on the back of the stove with exaggerated care, then followed Julia, helping her to close the remaining windows and bolt the shutters over them. The room grew dark as the last one was closed.

Julia hurried into the small bedroom opening off the main room of the house. She came back with two guns, one in each hand. Going back she returned this time with a powder horn, some wadding, and a pouch of lead balls. She glanced at Frankie but he was too engrossed with his play to have noticed anything but the change of light. To Sally, Julia said, "Light a lamp. The less he knows . . ."

Sally obediently lighted a lamp and placed it on the table near the stove. Her eyes were wide, her lips trembling as she whispered, "What did you see?"

Julia said, "Some birds flew up and the horses were all watching something down the draw."

"Maybe it was only a coyote. Or a deer."

Julia shook her head. "The horses are used to coyotes and deer."

Sally's voice was a frightened whisper. "Indians?"

"I think so. White men would have ridden right in openly."

"Maybe they only want some food."

"Or the horses. We'll just have to wait and see."

"What can we do if . . . ?" Sally didn't finish.

"We'll do the best we can," Julia said firmly. She knew she was the stronger of the two. Sally would probably get hysterical if the Indians tried to force their way into the house. She picked up one of the old smoothbore guns from the table. Both guns had attached ramrods. Julia removed one, poured powder into the muzzle of first one gun and then the other. She followed the powder with wadding, rammed it home with the ramrod, and after that dropped a ball into each muzzle. She followed those with more wadding and rammed it home too. Finished, she put the hammers of both guns on half cock and fitted a cap over each nipple. The guns were ready to fire now, but they were single-shot and there would be no time for reloading once the Indians got inside.

Julia was not a tall woman. She stood five feet four. She had large brown eyes, prominent cheekbones, and a strong chin and mouth. She was slender from the work she did around the ranch, but there was a bulge at her middle. She was five months pregnant with her first child. She laid a hand on her stomach, suddenly more terrified for the child than she was for herself.

Through the closed and barred windows she heard a commotion at the corral. She wished briefly that Clay and Tom Denton would suddenly come back. But they would not. They had been gone only three days and would probably be gone at least two weeks. Nobody expected Indians this far east, but as a precaution they had insisted that the two women stay together while they were gone. Now it looked as if that precaution had not been enough.

It had been a mistake to expect the Indians to stay farther west. They had harassed and mocked the troops at Fort Dodge less than fifty miles from here. Having successfully mocked the soldiers, they were more arrogant and dangerous than ever before. Some said it was conceivable they might even attack Dodge City itself in retaliation for the Sand Creek massacre four years ago.

Julia went to the window facing the corral. Cautiously and silently, she unbolted one shutter and opened it a crack.

What she saw confirmed her fears. There must have been a dozen painted, half-naked warriors in the yard and all of them had horses now. The corral gate was open and they were in the process of driving the Holleys' horses out. As she watched, one rode straight to the window and stared inside, meeting her glance from no more than three feet away.

Quickly she slammed the shutter and bolted it. But the damage had been done. They now knew there was at least one woman in the house. They wouldn't leave until she was in their hands.

Julia was trembling as she turned from the window. She called herself a fool for peering out, yet she knew it would probably have made no difference even if she had not. The Indians would have broken in to loot the place, regardless of who the occupants might be.

Now all they could do was wait. Julia thought about giving one gun to Sally then changed her mind. Frankie had noticed their fear and it was communicated to him. He began to cry and Sally went to try and comfort him. But it did no good. His mother's terror had become his own and until it was gone, his would not go away either.

The waiting seemed interminable. Faintly now Julia could hear the Indians' shrill whoops outside. Sometimes she heard one laugh. Sometimes she heard something shouted in the Indians' own tongue, something that drew a chorus of laughter from the others.

She felt the blood draining from her face. Without being able to understand their words, she knew what was being said and why they were laughing afterward. They were discussing the prize they knew awaited them inside the house. They didn't yet know there were two prizes here.

Suddenly all was quiet outside in the yard. Sally glanced at Julia, a wild hope having been born within her eyes. "They're gone," she whispered. "Oh thank God!"

Julia shook her head. She knew it was a ruse. She had not heard the thunder of horses hoofs which would have announced the departure of the Indians. They were only hoping those inside the house would believe they had gone and would open the barred door for them, thus making it unnecessary to go to all the work of forcing their way inside.

With one of the heavy muskets across her knees, she sat on the table, the other gun at her side, facing the door. She doubted if they'd try coming in the windows, but she knew if they did, she would hear the breaking glass in time to turn.

More waiting. More silence outside in the yard. Sally said, "They're gone. I'm going to look out and see."

There suddenly was steel in Julia Holley's voice. "Don't! They're still there! They're just waiting for us to open up and look."

Half an hour passed. Finally, Sally could stand the tension no more. Perhaps the incessant screaming of Frankie broke her nerve. She jumped to the floor and ran toward the door.

Julia was only a couple of feet behind. Sally laid a hand on the bar. With what seemed like brutality, Julia brought the gun muzzle down on her forearm as she did.

Sally shrieked with pain, but the bar stayed in place. She looked at Julia with stricken eyes and Frankie began to scream even louder than before.

Harshly Julia said, "Take care of him. I'll watch the door."

Sally, holding her hurt arm across her stomach, went to Frankie and knelt to take him in her arms. As she did, the first blow struck the door.

By the force of it, Julia knew they had one of the poles from the corral. Half a dozen blows would force the door, bar or no bar. Then they'd be in.

She knew what fate awaited her and Sally too. Repeated rape at the hands of the Indians. Abduction or death afterward. Frankie might not be killed, depending on the leader of the raiding party's mood. They all might be killed and left right here.

Julia faced the fact that the end had come. For her and for her unborn child. But she had two guns, both loaded. She clenched her jaws, firmed out her full and lovely mouth, and promised herself that two of the Indians were going to die in exchange for the deaths of her, her unborn child, and Sally and her boy.

Another shattering blow, and another, and now with each blow, the door shook. A hinge at the top tore loose, letting in the outside sunlight that cast a shaft of light across the floor.

Julia raised the gun. It was too heavy to hold steadily, so she got off the table, went around and crouched behind it, resting the gun muzzle on its top. The gun was steady now. She would hit whatever she aimed at.

She pulled the hammer back to full cock and slid the other gun over close so that she could get it easily. She thought briefly of her husband and thought of his agony when he found her dead, their unborn child dead inside of her.

Then the door crashed in, falling on the floor and raising a towering cloud of dust.

Sally screamed, "Don't shoot! Maybe they won't hurt us if we don't hurt them!"

Julia fired. Her sights had been squarely on the chest of the first Indian to come in. She hit him in the middle of his chest and the weight and force of the bullet drove him back into his comrades.

Julia snatched for the other gun. She thumbed back its hammer to full cock, took aim on the man behind the one she had shot, who was now on the floor. She fired again, just as Sally attempted to knock the muzzle of her gun aside.

Sally's gesture failed. The bullet struck the second Indian in the chest and he too was driven back.

For an instant, the doorway was clear of Indians. They had no way of knowing she had only had two guns, both of which were empty now. And for that brief instant, Julia dared to hope. Two dead Indians lay sprawled across the door sill. Maybe the others would leave.

But Sally was, by now, completely hysterical. Carrying Frankie, also screaming with terror, she ran out, climbing over the splintered door and stepping over the two Indians Julia had killed.

Outside, she was seized immediately. Her cries were silenced by a blow. Frankie was cuffed cruelly.

An Indian peered around the doorjamb and into the room. Julia was still crouched behind the table, the empty, smoking gun still in her hands.

The Indian came in with an unbelievable swift rush. He knocked her sprawling and seized the gun. Stunned, she felt herself being dragged outside.

The Indians loaded the bodies of their dead comrades. They went through the house, taking everything that suited their fancy, along with foodstuffs that might be useful to them later on. These they put into gunnysacks.

Julia had expected she and Sally would be raped and killed immediately. Instead they were boosted up on the horses that had been in the Holleys' corral, horses that the Indians saddled for them. Then, leading the horses upon which the women rode, the party of Indians rode away.

The last Indian inside the house overturned the kitchen stove. A plume of smoke came from the gaping kitchen door. It grew and grew, and by the time they went over the first rise, Julia, glancing back, could see flame where at first there had been only smoke.

When Clay returned, there would be nothing left. No house. No horses. No wife. He would come after her, of course. But what chance would he have? There were thousands of Indians within two hundred miles of here, and hundreds of different trails.

She had earlier resigned herself to death. The Indians were only waiting until they camped tonight, when they would have plenty of time and could savor what they intended doing to its fullest extent.

She glanced at Sally. Sally's face was numb, uncomprehending, as if her mind had snapped. And Frankie was asleep, whether from exhaustion or the blow, Julia couldn't tell.

CHAPTER
TWO

Clay Holley was a big man, six feet two, weighing 210 pounds, all of which was muscle and sinew and bone. He had a tawny mane of hair that saw the barber's shears maybe three times a year when he went to town. He wore a wide, cavalry-style mustache, as tawny as his hair, and except for that was normally clean-shaven. Right now, four weeks away from home, he had a heavy growth of whiskers on his face.

He and Tom Denton, slight, wiry, and dark, had delivered two hundred head of two- and three-year-old steers to the stockyards at Dodge. The money they had received for them, after paying off the loan, was in the bank in Dodge, except for enough to live on for a while, and in Clay's saddlebags was a new gown for Julia, with lace at the throat and sleeves, and some other things she had asked him to get. Grocery staples and canned goods were slung across the horse's rump in two gunnysacks, balancing each other and tied in place with the saddlestrings.

There was a new rifle, a Spencer repeater, thrust down into the scabbard on Clay's saddle. He wore his old Navy Colt's revolver at his waist, and, attached to the belt, was a battered powder horn and a pouch, containing wadding and bullets for the gun.

After a month away, he could hardly wait until he could hold Julia once more in his arms. He thought with great tenderness about the baby she was carrying.

He grinned faintly to himself. He had himself one hell of a woman. Strong and self-reliant and yet her beauty stayed in his mind, in his memory, even when he was far away from her. He could close his eyes and see her now. He could see the way her face would light up when she saw him coming. He could see the way she would run to him, and could almost feel the softness and warmth of her as she threw herself into his arms.

Another half mile now, and they'd top the last rise and be able to see the house. Tom Denton was grinning at him and he grinned back. And yet, unaccountably, some of the warmth seemed to have gone from the sky.

His spurs raked his horse's sides, and the animal broke into a lope. Grinning indulgently, Tom Denton spurred his own horse and kept pace behind.

Now the last rise lay ahead. Once over it, they would be able to see the house, the corral with its horses, the white chickens scratching in the yard, probably a clothesline of clean clothes drying in the breeze.

But when they topped the rise, that was not what they saw. The chickens were there, all right, and so was the corral, but empty with the gate ajar. The house itself was gone; only a pile of blackened embers on the ground remained.

Clay drew his revolver. His spurs raked the horse's sides repeatedly and savagely enough to draw blood.

The animal leaped ahead, running instantly, his belly low to the ground. But that was not enough for Clay. He slashed the horse's rump repeatedly with the barrel of the revolver, as if that could make the animal go faster than he already was.

Tom Denton wasn't more than fifty feet behind, his face as white and drawn as Clay's, his eyes as stricken.

Reaching the house, both men leaped from their horses while the animals were still at a run. Clay plunged toward the house, whose embers now were cold. He stared, saw nothing that resembled a body, then turned and ran for the sod barn. It was empty. So was the icehouse. So was the root cellar and so was the chickenhouse. Julia was gone. So was Sally Denton and so was the Dentons' little boy.

For a moment, Clay stood there, stunned, his mind absolutely refusing to work. He raised his glance and met Tom Denton's eyes. They were good friends despite differences in attitudes and the way they thought. Denton's eyes were filled with an intolerable pain that brought moisture to Clay Holley's eyes. He shook his head angrily. Grief accomplished nothing. This place had been attacked and burned. The first thing was to find who the attackers had been while the prints were still sufficiently plain upon the dusty ground. Next was to sift through the embers to make sure Julia and Sally and Frankie had not been burned to death.

Immediately he began circling the yard, searching the ground carefully with his glance. Two weeks had passed since the Indians had been here. There had been wind every day, but fortunately there had been no rain.

The tracks of unshod horses were everywhere. Coming out of the corral were the shod tracks of the three horses he had left for his wife's and Sally Denton's use. Nick and Duke, the buckboard team. And one saddle horse, his wife's, that she had named Buck.

From the number of tracks of unshod ponies, he guessed there must have been from six to a dozen Indians. He'd be better able to estimate the exact number later when he and Denton took the trail.

In front of the door there was still a deep gouge in the ground, sloughed by sun and time and wind, but still recognizable as having been made by someone being dragged. And he found one print, a plain one, of a woman's shoe.

He knew well what Indians did to captive white women. But in spite of that, his heart said a little prayer of thanks. They had not been slaughtered and burned right here. They were not inside the remains of the house.

Tom called to him and he hurried to where Denton stood. Denton pointed to the ground where several small tracks still were visible. Frankie's tracks. Clay said, "Let's go."

They returned to their horses and mounted them. Tom Denton hung back, letting Clay take the lead. Clay made a big circle of the place. He found the Indians had come up the draw afoot, leaving deep moccasin prints in the mud. He found where they had brought their horses in once they had satisfied themselves that no men were present here.

And at last he found the wide, plain trail through the waving prairie grass that the Indians had made when they left. Dismounting, he picked out the tracks of Nick and Duke and Buck, and, counting, decided there had been nearly a dozen of the Indians.

He knew what lay ahead. He knew that where the Indians had made camp that first night two weeks ago, they would probably find the bodies of Julia, Sally, and her son. The blood drained out of his face.

Now he held his horse to a more reasonable gait, a trot, because this was the only horse he had and he wasn't likely to obtain a change for a good many miles. He kept his eyes on the ground, on the trail in the prairie grass that had not yet disappeared, even after the passage of about two weeks. Occasionally they would cross a dry stream bed, or a dry wash, and here the trail would become plain and distinct.

Clay scowled fiercely, trying to keep his mind away from what he feared he was going to find ahead. Once, Tom Denton ranged up beside him and asked in a tight, strange voice, "What will they do to my boy? Will they . . . ?" He stopped. He had meant to ask, "Will they kill him too?" but had stopped, confused, not wanting to add anything to the agony Clay was going through.

Clay said, "They don't ordinarily kill kids. Likely they'll take him along and some family will take him and raise him with their own. Unless he cries too much or causes them too much trouble."

15

Denton said, "He'll be scared. He'll likely cry a lot."

"But he'll get tired."

Denton let his horse drop behind. Clay wondered what time of day the Indians had attacked and burned his house. He was trying to guess how much farther it would be to the Indians' first night's camp. Certainly their trail indicated they were in no hurry. Their horses had been walking. The arrogant bastards, he thought. They weren't even afraid of being pursued. And why should they be? The worst they could expect from that burned-out ranch back there was a pursuit by a few white men and they figured they could handle them easily.

For more than three years, ever since the Sand Creek massacre, both Arapahos and Cheyennes had been raiding ranches, white settlements, and stagecoach way stations. They had all but put a stop to the building of the railroad and the Army hadn't been able to put a stop to their raids. Their success made them even bolder and more daring.

Until now, Clay Holley, a fair man who could usually see both sides, had felt a certain sympathy for the Indians. Repeatedly they had been lied to and betrayed. The Sand Creek massacre had been a classic case in point. Promised protection by the commander of the nearby Army post. Cheyennes under Black Kettle and a few Arapahos had camped on Sand Creek.

Troops of volunteers under Colonel Chivington had marched through winter snow and, one morning at dawn, had attacked the sleeping village without warning of any kind. Men, women, and children were slaughtered indiscriminately. Most of the casualties the white men suffered were inflicted by their own comrades in the frenzy of undirected firing.

Far from accomplishing its purpose to subjugate and pacify the Indians, the massacre had exactly the opposite effect. One of the sons of William Bent, who had taken a Cheyenne wife, was present at the scene but managed to escape. Thereafter, he led a band of savage Cheyenne dog soldiers that terrorized the frontier for many months.

And it still was going on. But when it is a man's own family that is called upon to pay for a slaughter in which neither he nor any of his family had a part, sympathy fades and fury takes its place. Clay Holley would follow the Indians that had kidnapped his pregnant wife and the wife and child of Tom Denton. If they had killed the captives, he would exact a bloody revenge. If the captives were still alive, he would not rest until he had rescued them.

It was now late afternoon. The sun hung low in the western sky, staining the few high clouds a brilliant gold and orange. And suddenly Clay rode down into a narrow, brush-grown stream bed, and straight into the site of the Indians' camp.

Horse tracks had almost pounded what little grass there was into the ground. The remains of several fires were visible. There were places that had been hollowed out by the Indians to accommodate their hip bones while they slept.

Like a hound with a fresh scent, Clay Holley quested about the camp, bent over, his face cold and intent.

Tom Denton, less sure of himself in matters involving tracking, followed uncertainly.

Into the cold, intent eyes of Clay Holley, a little hope began to grow. He had found no bodies, and if the Indians had not killed their captives the first night, there was a chance they had not killed them at all.

Why? That was a question for which no answer came to him. Young Frankie Denton might have been spared simply because he was a child and Indians have as much affection for children as anyone. His own wife might have been spared because she was so plainly carrying a child herself. But sparing Sally Denton puzzled him. Unless one of the Indians had decided he wanted her for his squaw, a possibility because of her yellow hair.

He straightened, having circled the Indian camp beyond the point where there were any tracks, except those made riding to this place and those made riding away. There still was pain in his eyes; there still was strain on his face. But there was also a faint look of satisfaction too. He said, "They didn't kill 'em the first night, anyway."

"Did they . . . ?"

Denton knew what he meant and the smile disappeared from his mouth. "Likely did. I can't tell because it's been so long. But they didn't kill 'em and now it isn't likely that they will."

"Maybe they'd just as well be dead."

"Not my Julia. I want my Julia alive no matter what's happened to her or what's going to happen to her."

Tom Denton's eyes were tortured as he thought of what must have happened here in this spot two weeks ago. He met Clay's glance and he had the grace to look ashamed. He said, "I do too, I guess, only it's killing me to think about it. In front of the boy and all."

Clay's voice was harsh and held no sympathy. "Then don't think about it. Come on. 'We'll camp on the other side of the stream."

They remounted and splashed their horses across the narrow, shallow stream, stopping in the middle to let the horses drink. On the other side they unsaddled, picketed the horses, and built a small fire. Having been on roundup, they had blankets and cooking utensils. Clay had two gunnysacks of food he had been bringing home from Dodge.

Silently, with no talk, they made coffee, cooked bacon, and fried unleavened dough in the grease. They ate as silently as they had prepared the meal, and afterward scattered the fire, got their blankets, and lay down to sleep. But neither man could sleep. Clay Holley lay awake, his eyes on the millions of stars overhead, and thought of Julia. Julia was strong. They wouldn't break her easily.

But Sally Denton was something else. Tom had been Sally's strength. Without him, there would be little to carry her through the ordeal that lay ahead.

Tom's voice came from the darkness, almost inaudible. "How far will they take them, do you think?"

"To wherever their village is."

"We're already up against ten or twelve. What are we going to do when they get to their village and we have forty or fifty to go up against?"

Clay Holley didn't want to think about that. He was damned if he was going to lie here sleepless inventing obstacles. With little patience, he replied, "We'll think about that when it happens and not until. Right now we've got a lot of catching up to do. And if we don't get some sleep, we're not going to be in any shape for catching anything."

Tom Denton did not reply. Clay closed his eyes determinedly. He slept eventually but only after a miserable, sleepless hour had dragged slowly by.

CHAPTER
THREE

They were up at dawn and on the trail again. The horses, having had a full night's rest and plenty of grass to eat, were eager to go. Clay Holley let them lope for nearly an hour, until they slowed down of their own free will. They had sweated some, so he held them to a trot, letting them cool off. Two weeks had passed since the attack. He wouldn't hesitate to kill both these horses in the pursuit, but he wouldn't do it needlessly. The two weeks' gap in time couldn't be closed in a day or two.

All day they rode, cheered at noon to discover the second night's camp of the Indians. Once more, Holley quested about the camp, looking for whatever he could find. He found a goodly number of footprints made by Frankie Denton. He found two different sets of woman's shoe prints so he knew both women were still alive, still able to get around. He found the prints of all three shod horses the Indians had stolen from the corral, Nick, Duke, and Buck.

From the size of the fires' remains, he judged that the Indians had camped early and had broken camp late. They were in no hurry. They had no doubt looted the Holley house before they burned it, and were pleased with the loot they had obtained. Having no destination but their home village, and nothing particular to do when they arrived, they were loafing across the plain, something Holley found very heartening.

At sundown, they found another of the Indians' camps. Going on, they traveled until they could no longer make out the trail. Another small fire and another quick meal, and tonight they went to sleep without delay.

Next morning, they came upon the fourth Indian camp; Holley spent nearly half an hour scouting this one. He found part of the carcass of a deer. He found twice the usual number of fires. He found enough footprints so that he knew this was a camp that had been here several days. Riding out to where the horse herd had been held, he studied the close-cropped grass and the area it covered, and, knowing the approximate number of horses the Indians had, judged they had remained here at least three days.

Elated, he returned to Denton. "They stayed here at least three days." Without noticing the expression on Denton's face, he rode out, made a big circle, and finally found the trail the Indians had made leaving here. One of the horses was dragging a travois. Clay tried to guess what the travois had been loaded with. One of the women, injured or sick and unable to ride a horse? A deer they had killed and had not been able to consume? He had no idea.

Denton, following him, saw the scratches made in the ground by the travois poles. His face turned red with anger. "The bastards have hurt them so bad they can't even ride anymore."

Clay Holley shook his head. "I don't think so. The rule among these Plains Indians is that the woman belongs to everybody the first night. After that, she belongs just to the one that captured her. So they're not being gang-raped every night. Because she's with child, maybe Julia hasn't been touched at all. At least, they're both alive. And if they've been kept alive this long, the Indians aren't likely to kill them now."

"But riding every day, all day. And being treated like that at night . . ."

"They're not riding hard all day. They were in that last camp at least three days. And don't run either Julia or Sally down. They're ranch women and they're tough. They know as soon as we got back we came after them. They're going to stay alive until we can rescue them."

"I wish to God I had your faith."

"Faith is all we got. Now shut up and let's get on with it."

They rode out again, with Holley not missing the extremely leisurely pace at which the Indians were traveling. Dismounting in one spot, where the trail crossed a dry and sandy riverbed, he guessed they had narrowed the distance separating them to about four days. It looked as if whenever the Indians felt like it, they stopped to hunt.

The Indians seemed to have no fear. They built fires at night and Holley could find no signs of sentries being put out to guard against surprise attack. But they were still ten or twelve against two. And the instant they were attacked, they would kill their three captives with neither mercy nor hesitation.

That was what really bothered Clay. He wasn't afraid of attacking whatever number of Indians they were following. He knew Tom Denton would be as ruthless and efficient as he himself would be.

They were now south of the Kansas line. They were in Indian Territory, but the land looked much the same. Rolling hills, covered with waving grass, and with short, curly buffalo grass native to these plains. Mountains raised their blue summits in the distance. There were bluffs, with rock rims and flat table tops, and there were dry gulches carved in the plain by flash floods over hundreds and maybe thousands of years past.

A couple of times they spotted buffalo in the distance, black, scattered spots upon the plain. Once they came to a place where the Indians they were following had pursued, killed, and butchered a buffalo. The head with its massive horns remained along with a large area where blood had soaked the ground, and a pile of entrails that even the Indians could not use. Hide, meat, liver, heart, and kidneys had been carried away, probably on the travois because the gouges in the ground were much deeper now.

Clay Holley wasted little time at the site. To him, the buffalo slaughter meant delay on the part of the Indians. It meant that when he and Denton left this spot they would be that much closer to them.

Sometimes, as he rode, he tried to plan the strategy they would use when they caught up. But the best plan eluded him. They were two against ten or twelve.

Whatever attack they made would have to depend upon complete surprise. They had to watch out for their own safety, too, or both of them might die in the attempt, and if they did, all hope would end for Julia and Sally Denton and the boy.

Two more days passed and at last, on the afternoon of the third, they crossed a wash in which there was some dry sand. Clay dismounted to study the tracks. Now, instead of being read in days, the signs were only hours old and damned few hours at that.

He had little idea, by now, of where they were, Indian Territory still, perhaps. Maybe even Texas. Certainly they were far south of the Kansas line. But it mattered little where they were because they could expect no help from anyone. All they could hope for was to catch up with this party of Indians before they reached their main village.

Now Clay Holley traveled more cautiously, careful that their horses raised no dust, careful too to keep their mounts in the shallow valleys so that never could they and their horses be silhouetted upon the top of a ridge.

He dismounted frequently to study the Indians' tracks. At about four in the afternoon he held his hand close to some horse droppings and detected warmth. Sure now that the Indians could be no more than half a mile ahead, he handed his horse's reins to Tom and walked to the top of the next shallow rise. He got down and crawled the last thirty or forty feet. When his head topped the rise, and he could see, he felt a fierce satisfaction. There, less than a quarter mile ahead, were the Indians. He counted swiftly. There were only nine, fewer than he had thought.

Quickly he spotted Nick, pulling the travois. Duke was carrying Sally Denton, the boy in front of her. Julia . . . his eyes clung to her hungrily. Julia was riding her own saddle horse, Buck. She rode astride, her skirts pulled up to make that possible. Even from this distance he could see how ragged her dress was, could see how badly it was torn. Her hair was braided, probably the only way she could keep it out of her face and eyes with no comb and no opportunity to care for it properly.

But she was alive! And she appeared to be all right. He couldn't tell from this distance whether she still carried her unborn child or not. Raw fury touched him. If she wasn't, every one of the nine Indians would pay with his life.

He crawled back down to where Tom Denton waited with the horses. He said, "They're a quarter mile ahead."

"Is Sally . . . ?"

"Sally's all right and so is Frankie. So is Julia, I think, although I couldn't tell at that distance whether her child was all right or not."

"What are we going to do?"

"The only thing we can. We'll hit their camp tonight, after they've settled down to sleep."

"What's to keep them from killing the women?"

"I figure they'll be surprised. And we can yell at the women to run."

"It's risky. For the women and Frankie I mean."

26

Wryly Clay asked, "You got a better idea?"

Tom Denton shook his head.

"All right then, we'll do it that way." He sat down on the ground and looked up at Tom. "We'd just as well stay here. No use taking the chance of being seen. Not when we're this close to them. We'll move at dark, or a little before so we can still see their trail. At the rate they're traveling they're not likely to go much more than five miles before they camp."

Denton got down. He dropped the reins of both horses so that they could graze, but he didn't take the bits out of their mouths. They needed to be ready to move and move quickly if another bunch of Indians surprised them.

Denton's face wore a worried frown. Clay felt as worried as Denton, but he didn't let it show. He knew the odds. They were up against nine Indians, who would kill Frankie and the women before they'd let them be rescued. The only hope Clay and Denton had was to kill so many of them in the first volley that the rest would flee.

If that happened, maybe they could rescue the women. But even if they did, they still had the remaining Indians to contend with. Furthermore there might be other Indians in the vicinity, and they could no doubt be summoned quickly and easily. And a hundred and fifty or two hundred miles lay between here and the safety of Dodge City or Fort Dodge.

He turned his face away from Denton so that Tom wouldn't see how worried he really was. The truth was, there was little chance of pulling the rescue off successfully, and even less of getting away. But there wasn't any other way.

The sun sank lower in the sky with maddening slowness. Clay kept his eyes moving, searching ridge tops, but nothing appeared. At last the sun dipped behind one of those ridge tops and Clay got to his feet. He said, "I think we can move now if we go slow and try to keep from being silhouetted against the sky."

Denton mounted immediately. He also had a Spencer, holding seven shots. Between them, they had enough firepower to kill all of the Indians, even allowing for a miss or two. The trouble was, the light was going to be bad. The Indians would be moving. And they'd have to worry about the safety of the captives.

At the crest of the first ridge, he stared ahead. The sky was flaming now. In the distance he saw a rise of dust and knew it was caused by the Indians and their captives, now about five miles away.

Immediately he dropped down into a draw and followed it until it petered out. By then, the sky was gray and there was little chance of their being seen. He returned to the Indians' trail and followed it until it was too dark to see. Then, taking a bearing on a star, he lifted his horse to a steady trot, with Denton keeping pace immediately behind.

The five miles took about an hour to ride and by the time they crested the last rise and brought the Indians' campfires into sight, it was completely dark, the only light being that given off by the stars in the cloudless sky.

Clay Holley dismounted about a quarter mile from the camp, making sure that there was a crosswind blowing between them and the Indian camp. That would ensure that the Indians' horses would not smell theirs and that their horses would not smell those of the Indians.

It disturbed him that there were so many fires down below. He counted six in all, and he couldn't understand why nine Indians, with two women captives and a boy, would need six fires. Not when a couple would have done.

The two crept forward silently. Both had their Spencer repeaters in their hands and it occurred to Clay, now that it was much too late, that if he had left Julia the Spencer or even the revolver instead of those two old muzzle-loaders, she might now be safe back there at home. Guilt flooded him briefly, but then he thought that none of them had really expected Indians to be that far east, and having the women stay together had been more for the sake of companionship than safety.

Not until they were three hundred yards from the Indian camp did Clay realize that there were now more than nine Indians down below. He felt a sudden hollowness in his chest, and an empty feeling in his belly. They were one day late. Counting, he realized that there were at least double the original number of Indians in the camp below. Any chance of rescuing the women had all but disappeared.

As if he blamed Clay, Tom Denton said, "They've joined up with another bunch. There's twice as many of them down there now."

Clay did not reply. He was thinking that two men, even armed with Spencer repeaters and revolvers, had no chance against that many Indians. Particularly when the lives of their wives and of Denton's son were at stake. They had no choice but to go back to get help.

He searched the camp until his eyes found his wife. She came from the darkness carrying an armload of wood. He squinted his eyes and stared until she turned a certain way, silhouetting herself in side view and he was able to see the bulge in her middle. Thank God, he thought. They haven't hurt her enough to make her lose the child.

In silence they lay there, watching the Indian camp. The Indians cooked meat on sticks over the fires, the women cooked their own. Afterward the Indians talked for a time, and once one of them got up and did an impromptu war dance around one of the fires.

Eventually, though, the fires died. The Indians scattered and lay down to sleep. Clay watched the two women intently, marking in his mind exactly where they were when they settled down to sleep.

There was agonizing doubt in his thoughts. He and Denton had come at least a hundred and fifty miles, tracking their stolen wives. Now they could see them, less than a quarter mile away. But to try and rescue them was to place them in deadly jeopardy because the first thing Indians do when caught with white captives is to put them to death.

And yet, how could they leave their wives and Denton's son in the Indians' hands? That was a question for which there was no answer in Clay Holley's mind.

CHAPTER
FOUR

So far, Clay Holley had been, involuntarily, the leader of this two-man expedition, maybe because he was more experienced in tracking, maybe because his was the stronger of the two personalities. But Tom Denton had as much to lose as he had and was entitled to a voice in whatever decision was made.

In the darkness, he glanced at Tom's blurred face. "You've got as much to say about this as I do. What do you want to do? If we get ourselves killed, that's the end of all hope for your wife and mine. Both our kids will be raised as Indians. On the other hand, if we leave now and go back, we might never be able to find them again, even if we can get the Army to send an expedition after them. There's a third possibility. If we make an attack and get the Indians excited, they might kill both women before we can get them away."

Tom Denton was silent for several moments. At last he said, "You know more about this than I do. What do you think we ought to do?"

Clay frowned in the darkness. It was a question he had been trying to decide for himself, so now he spoke his thoughts aloud. "I think we ought to wait until the Indians are asleep. Then I think we ought to go in and try to get the women out without stirring up a hornets' nest. If the Indians wake up and it turns into a fight, we'd better get the hell out and go back to Dodge. I don't want to be the cause of my wife's getting killed, or yours either. I don't want revenge near as much as I want Julia back alive."

"I don't know whether I can go back without Sally and my boy."

"Well, you'd better think about that before we head down into that Indian camp, because I don't think we've got one chance in fifty of pulling it off. And if we don't, you either go back to Dodge without your wife or you stay right here, dead."

Again there was a silence, this one lasting longer than the earlier one. At last Tom Denton said, reluctantly, "All right."

"All right what?"

"If we fail and live through it, I'll go back to Dodge with you."

Clay Holley felt a touch of satisfaction. He had feared Denton might give him trouble about leaving. He didn't want to leave any more than Denton did, but if they roused the Indians, their only chance of survival lay in flight. And the quicker they got away, the better chance of survival the women had.

He said, "It's settled then. One of us has got to get to the women and your boy, wake them, and get them away without rousing the Indians. The other has got to get to the Indians' pony herd and run them off. Pick your job. It makes no difference to me."

Denton thought a moment. "You get the women. I'll run the horses off."

"All right. But you'll have to catch one of the Indian horses to ride. I'll need both of ours. Think you can do it?"

"I can do it."

"And run the Indians' horses at least until daylight. We don't want them able to come after us. Go straight north, and I'll locate you by the dust at dawn."

Denton grunted agreement. Clay Holley thought it was a good plan, as good as could be devised. Maybe it would work and maybe it would not, but at least, afterward, they'd know they had thought it out and done their best, no matter what happened as a result.

Below, the fires gradually died until gray ash covered most of their glow. A couple of hours after the Indians had bedded down, Holley said, "All right, let's go. Circle around. The horses are on the far side of the camp. There'll be at least one and maybe two Indians watching them, maybe young ones or even boys. Don't waste any sympathy on them no matter what their age. Kill them or knock them out but be damn sure they don't make any noise."

"The horses are going to make some noise."

Clay Holley thought about that a moment. "Get yourself in position. Then count to a hundred and fifty. But if you hear any racket in the Indian camp back here before that, drive them off right away."

"All right." Denton unexpectedly stuck out his hand and Holley gripped it. It was a good-bye handshake and both men understood. Both knew the risk involved in what they were going to do. Both knew the chance of ever seeing each other alive again was slim.

Denton moved away into the darkness and disappeared. Holley took a moment to tie the reins of one horse to the other's tail and to tie the reins of the first horse to a clump of brush, so he'd know exactly where both of them were when he needed them. He waited a few moments more to give Denton time to circle the Indian camp. Then, as silently as any Indian, despite his run-down-at-the-heel Texas boots, he moved down the slight grassy slope toward the Indian camp.

He had the location of the two women and Denton's boy firmly fixed in his mind and headed straight toward it.

Every nerve and muscle in his body was tense. He muttered a short, fervent prayer, not for himself but for Julia and, belatedly and a little ashamedly, for Sally Denton and her son. Now he was an eighth of a mile from the Indian camp. Now he was a short hundred yards. And suddenly one of the Indians sat up, stretched, got up and went to one of the fires to stir it with a stick and add wood to it.

Holley cursed angrily beneath his breath. He held the Spencer in both hands, a cartridge in the chamber. He could kill the Indian but doing so would be self-defeating. It would rouse the others and kill all chance of accomplishing what they had set out to do.

Nor did he have the time to wait until the Indian lay down and went back to sleep. Tom Denton was already on the other side of the Indian camp. Unless he too could see the Indian who had wakened and gotten up,

35

he would go ahead with his plan to stampede and drive away the Indian pony herd.

Holley took a couple of steps closer to the Indian camp. A twig snapped beneath his foot. The Indian at the fire turned his head and stared into the darkness. Holley knew he could not be seen but he also knew the Indian had been alerted by the sound.

Suddenly on the far side of the camp, Holley heard a shout. It was followed almost instantly by the roar of a rifle. Denton's Spencer, Holley knew. There was the thunder of horses' hoofs, another rifle shot, and then Indians were running everywhere, most toward where the horses had been, others toward Holley. The Indian at the fire had pointed in Holley's direction, snatched a gun, and begun to run toward him.

No longer, Holley knew, was there the slightest chance of rescuing the women. All he could hope now was that pursuing him and Denton would occupy them and keep them from killing Julia, Sally, and the boy.

He turned and sprinted for the place he had left the horses, with the Indians less than fifty yards behind. A volley of shots rang out on the far side of the camp, mingling with the thunder of the running horses' hoofs. Holley reached the horses, swiftly untied the reins of his own horse from the clump of brush, and swung to the animal's back.

The Indians had stopped running and were shooting blindly. One of their bullets struck Denton's horse, running behind and still tied to the tail of Holley's horse. He went down instantly. His reins, tied to the tail of Holley's horse, pulled out a good-sized clump of hair and Holley's horse let out a squeal of pain. But the pain made him run even faster than before. The Indians, their camp, even the flashes and roaring of the guns faded and, as Holley went over a rise, completely disappeared.

Holley had never cursed so angrily in his life before. He had been within fifty yards of Julia, Sally, and the boy, and he might as well have been fifty miles for all the good it did. They had failed. They had followed these Indians for a week and they had failed. Furthermore they had endangered the lives of both women and the boy. The only hope was that the Indians were so busy chasing them that nobody would bother killing the captives. By the time the Indians returned to camp, they would know only two white men had been involved. They could read tracks better than any white man could.

Holley kept his horse at a lope, listening for the sound of the Indian horse herd on his left. Hearing it, he veered left to join up with Tom Denton and help him out.

His horse leaped gullies and avoided rocks that Holley didn't even see. The sound of the galloping Indian horse herd grew louder.

No longer did it make good sense to drive the Indian horse herd until daylight. Sally Denton, Julia, and Sally's boy were completely at the Indians' mercy. To anger them unnecessarily would only further endanger the captives' lives.

He brought the first of the galloping Indian horse herd into sight and slowed his own mount slightly so that he could join Tom Denton at the rear. After several minutes, he spotted a rider on one of the horses and closed quickly with him.

Almost immediately he realized Tom was hurt. His friend clung to the horse's neck, encircling it with both arms, slumped over the horse's withers. He wasn't driving the horses. He was only hanging onto his own mount, which was running after the others.

Clay yelled, "Tom? You hit?"

He got no reply, but Tom Denton did turn his head.

It was too dark to see Tom Denton's face, too dark to know what expression it held. Clay shouted, "Can you hold on? For just a little longer?"

He was closer now, riding side by side with Tom Denton's horse, and he saw Tom nod his head. Again he cursed angrily to himself. Maybe if the group of Indians they were trailing had not, tonight, joined up with a larger group, they might have brought it off. Or if that damned Indian hadn't picked that particular time to get up and replenish one of the fires . . .

But it was done and they had failed. And Tom was plainly wounded, perhaps very seriously judging from the way he looked.

How much farther should they go, Clay asked himself, before he dared stop and tend Tom Denton's wounds? Suddenly he decided this was far enough. The Indians were afoot. It would take them half an hour to catch up. That would give him fifteen minutes to tend Tom's wounds, another fifteen minutes to get a lead on the Indians. Probably they wouldn't even bother to pursue.

Leaning far over, he tossed the loop of his lariat over the head of the Indian pony Tom was riding. He drew both horses to a gradual halt so that a sudden stop wouldn't break Tom's hold on his horse's mane.

Once both horses were stopped, he dallied the rope around the saddle horn, dismounted instantly, went to Tom, and eased him from the saddle. He laid him gently on the ground. Tom seemed to be only semiconscious, and he asked urgently, "Where are you hit?"

Close now, he could see the froth of blood and bubbles coming from Tom's mouth. It told him Tom was hit in the chest. It told him too that Tom was close to death. There was no way on earth Tom could travel the hundreds of miles back to Kansas where they'd started from.

Tom asked weakly, his words widely spaced because of his rapidly waning strength, "Did you get them? Are Sally and Frankie safe?"

Clay started to tell him the truth, then closed his mouth. When he opened it again, he said, "They're all right. I sent them on ahead."

Tom began to cough. When he stopped coughing, he managed to choke out the words, "Thank God." And then he died. His chest was still, his breathing stopped.

Clay gathered him up in his arms. He laid him across the Indian pony, which fidgeted and tried to get away. He cut off the end of his lariat and with it tied Tom's hands and feet beneath the belly of the horse. He was damned if he was going to leave Tom's body for the

Indians to mutilate in front of Sally and Julia and the boy.

Then, ignoring the scattering herd of Indian ponies, he mounted his own horse and leading the one to which Tom was tied, rode north again, maintaining a trot in the hope that by the time the Indians recovered their horses and it got light, he would have enough of a lead so that they'd not be able to catch up with him, or wouldn't think it worth their while. He'd bury Tom as soon as he was sure he was in the clear.

Never in his life had Clay Holley felt so defeated, so helpless. He and Tom had failed miserably and Tom had lost his life. He had no idea what to do next.

What he did know was that he had no intention of giving up. He would find some way to rescue Julia, Sally, and Tom Denton's boy and would continue his efforts until he had them home safely or until he lost his own life in the attempt.

CHAPTER
FIVE

Clay Holley rode north at a steady trot for half a day. Each time he crested a rise, he turned around in his saddle and stared behind, looking for the telltale lift of dust that would tell him he was being pursued. Several times he stopped and studied the land to the south carefully. He saw nothing and at last, near noon, concluded that the Indians had recovered their ponies, given up the idea of pursuit, and turned back.

He thought of Julia, thought what her state of mind must be, knowing he had been so close, knowing he had failed and, finally, thinking he had abandoned his effort to rescue her.

Would she believe herself abandoned by him for good? He could not believe she would. She knew how he loved her and how he longed for their baby's birth. And yet, there would inevitably be times when her faith would falter, when her hope would fail.

He considered, rashly, going back as soon as he had buried Tom. But he put the thought quickly away. His purpose was to rescue her, and to rescue Sally and Frankie Denton along with her, not to die uselessly in a vain attempt to prove to her he had not abandoned her.

She would know that eventually even if she could not wholly believe it now.

He went on and finally, in midafternoon, halted, dismounted and eased Tom's body off the Indian horse to the ground at the edge of a deep gully that floods had cut across the plain.

He had no shovel and without one, no way in which to dig Tom a grave. Too many days of hot sun lay between here and Dodge City to consider taking Tom's body back. But he could lay Tom's body in the bottom of the wash and cave in enough earth to cover him and protect his body from the ravages of vultures and wolves.

He laid Tom at the edge of the wash, then descended into it, climbed the side and lifted the body in. He couldn't help wondering, now, if Tom had killed any of the Indians during his theft of the horse herd. He had heard Tom's gun firing and Tom didn't usually miss. But it had been dark. Clay hoped Tom's shots had all missed their marks. If no Indians had been killed, then the women's chances of survival were much better than if they had.

He closed Tom's eyes and crossed his hands upon his chest. He climbed back out of the wash, and with his feet, caved the edge of the wash down into it. He kept working until he guessed at least three feet of earth covered Tom. Then he made a full circle with his glance, memorizing the landmarks so that he could find this spot again for Sally and for Tom Denton's son. He took a full half hour gathering rocks to make a mound three feet high at the edge of the wash. Then, sweating heavily from the effort, he mounted his horse and, trailing the barebacked Indian pony, once more headed north.

Clay was not a religious man, but it suddenly occurred to him that he had buried Tom with no ceremony, without even a blessing. He returned to the side of the wash, dismounted, and stared down at the fresh earth covering the body of his friend. He said awkwardly, "I'm not much at praying, but I knew you, and you were a good man. I don't guess there's much doubt about where you'll end up. But if it'll make you rest any easier, I'll promise you one thing: I won't give up. I'll stay with it until my wife and yours and Frankie are free again or until I'm dead."

He turned away, mounted again, and once more headed north. And now his mind began to consider ways in which he could accomplish the rescue of the two women and the boy.

Trying to negotiate for their release through the reservation Indian agents seemed to him to be a futile and dangerous course. Before admitting to their agent that they had white captives, the Cheyennes would probably get rid of them. Besides, the Cheyennes weren't listening to their agents now and wouldn't, at least until winter immobilized them and drove them to the agencies, where they could get food for their ponies and for themselves during the winter months.

There appeared to be only two other alternatives. One was to try persuading the military to mount a campaign against the Cheyennes. The other lay in trying to recruit enough white men to effect the rescue without the help of the military.

The second course would take money. A lot of it. He either would have to borrow that money from the bank in Dodge, using his ranch and cattle as security, or would have to sell both the cattle and the ranch.

Borrowing would be the quickest course. So he'd try that first. Selling might take a lot of time, time he didn't have.

He camped, and went on, and camped again the following night. During the daylight hours when he was traveling, he kept his eyes moving, studying the ground for fresh trails and the skyline for Indians. He crossed many trails, none of them fresh.

He resisted stubbornly the compulsion to push his horse beyond the animal's endurance. Killing the animal would cost him much time in the end. Besides, he had long since told himself that haste in this situation was absolutely impossible. He would encounter resistance from the Army, perhaps outright refusal. He doubted if, with hostiles roaming the plains at will, the Dodge City bank would loan him any substantial sum on his cattle and his ranch. He faced the likelihood that anyone willing to buy his ranch would pay far less than it was worth. And lastly, recruiting men willing to ride against the Indians when the odds were perhaps fifty to one would be no easy task.

And yet, somehow he would manage it. Somehow he would ride south again with a sufficient force to rescue his wife, Sally Denton, and her son. He never once let himself have any doubt of that.

A week after burying Tom Denton, he struck the Arkansas. Not knowing whether he was east or west of Dodge City, he followed the river east awhile, until it took a sharp turn toward the north. He knew then that he was well east of Dodge, and so reversed his direction of travel and headed west.

The sun went down and dusk darkened the sky. But tonight, Clay Holley kept going until, near midnight, he rode into Dodge.

He took his two horses to the livery stable, where he put them into stalls. He fed them some hay himself, since the hostler had long since gone to sleep. Carrying his saddlebags, he walked up the dark and silent street to the hotel.

Not once, since leaving her in the hands of the Indians, had his thoughts left Julia. Now, heading toward the hotel in the quiet darkness, he thought again, as he had so many times in the last week, of Julia, lying in the arms of some savage who had taken her as one of his wives, and the pain of that thought was nearly unendurable. It made him want to shriek out his protest at the sky. And yet, even in his pain, he knew he would rather have her in some Indian's lodge than dead. Even though she had been taken as some Indian's squaw, she still belonged to him, in her heart and mind, in her body. The child she was carrying was his. And no matter what happened between now and the time he rescued her, they could go back to the way it had been before. No Indian, no tribe of Indians could deny him that.

He reached the hotel and went inside. There was a veranda in front on which were several empty chairs. There was a single lamp burning behind the desk, and a bell on the desk. Holley brought his hand down on the top of it, ringing it. He had to ring three times before a sleepy-eyed man in a long nightshirt came from a room behind the desk.

He looked grouchily at Clay and shoved the register at him. Clay signed and the man shoved a key at him. "Third door on the right at the top of the stairs. Try and be quiet about it. It's late."

Clay nodded. He took the key and, carrying his saddlebags, mounted the stairs. Only one lamp was burning along the entire length of the hall. It was almost completely dark, but he had no trouble finding the right door. He unlocked it, went in and struck a match. He lighted the lamp on the table, then closed and locked the door.

He was tired, very tired. But worse than his weariness was the feeling of emptiness. Everything that had made his life worthwhile was gone. His wife. His friend Tom Denton and Denton's wife and son. His ranch house and everything it had contained.

Numbly he sat down on the edge of the bed and took off his boots. He slipped out of his shirt and pants after hanging his revolver and belt over the back of a chair. He leaned his rifle against the wall beside the bed.

He blew out the lamp and crawled into bed. The window was open and a soft breeze out of the east stirred the dirty curtains and brought in the night noises of the sleeping town, the bark of a dog, the hoofbeats of a saddle horse in the street out front, the slamming of a door.

Lying awake in the darkness, he found himself thinking of Julia again. He forced himself to stop. Torturing himself would accomplish nothing, and down underneath, Clay Holley was a practical man. He was doing all he could. He would continue doing all he could.

The rescue, which must motivate his life from now until he succeeded, was going to take time, a lot of time. Weeks, maybe months, maybe even years.

He would not desist until he had succeeded in rescuing Julia, Sally Denton, and her son, or until he had verified their deaths. He closed his eyes.

Exhausted as he was, it still took more than half an hour for him to go to sleep. When he awakened, the first rays of the morning sun were streaming into the window.

He got up, dressed, and poured cold water from the pitcher on the washstand into the wash pan. After washing, he shaved carefully for the first time in weeks. He combed his hair, settled his hat on his head, then buckled on his gun. Leaving the rifle in the room along with his saddlebags, he locked the door as he went out.

Clay had some friends in Dodge and Tom Denton's brother lived here. He knew he had to see Frank, however unpleasant that chore might be. He went out through the lobby and headed for the small two-room house down on the bank of the Arkansas where Frank Denton lived.

He walked the length of the street and beyond along a two-track road to the river's edge. It wasn't hard to find Frank Denton's house. Denton was just coming from the outhouse as Clay strode into the yard.

He had met Frank Denton a couple of times while he and Tom Denton had been in Dodge to ship cattle, and Frank recognized him. "What are you doing back in Dodge? You just left a couple of weeks ago."

Clay said, "I've got bad news. When we got home to my place where we'd left the women, they were gone. The house had been burned to the ground."

"Been burned? You mean it wasn't an accident?" Frank's face was shocked.

Clay said, "Indians. Nine of them."

"Oh my God! Are the women dead? And Frankie too?"

"Kidnapped, not dead."

"Didn't you go after them?"

Clay stared at him angrily. "Hell, yes, we went after them! Where do you think I've been the last two weeks? We found them too, but only after the nine that took them had been joined by more. Tom was shot running their horses off. I never got near the women."

"Where is Tom? Is he hurt bad?" The succession of shocks had turned Frank Denton's face almost gray.

He had the same facial characteristics that Tom had possessed, but physically he was as different as night from day. He was short, stocky, strong as a bull, and must have weighed half again as much as had his brother Tom.

48

Clay said, "He died of his wound. He was shot in the chest. I buried him a week south of here."

"Oh good God!"

Clay said, "There's a good chance that Sally and Frankie are still alive. My wife too. Unless Tom killed some of the Indians before they shot him."

"And you just left them there? In the hands of those murderin' redskins?"

Clay stifled his feeling of angry irritation. He asked, "What would you have done, charged in there and got yourself killed? What good would that have done them?"

Frank insisted furiously, "Hell, you were right there. You could have done something!"

"What? What could I have done? I figured if one of us ran off the horses, maybe the other could get the women away. Only it didn't work. Tom had to shoot to get the horses away, and the shots roused the whole damn camp."

Frank grumbled, "Come on in the house. I've got some coffee on."

Clay knew there would be no more recriminations. The initial shock had worn off along with the natural need to blame somebody. He followed Frank into the house, which was as untidy as most bachelor places were.

The pair sat at the table drinking coffee that tasted terrible. Finally Frank asked, "What now? What are we going to do?"

Clay felt encouraged that Frank had so naturally included himself in whatever plans might develop for rescuing Julia and Tom Denton's wife and son. He said, "The first thing I thought of was going to the Indian Bureau and trying to get them back through the Indian agent on the reservation. I decided that would probably be the worst thing possible, because the Indians would kill all three before they'd admit to having them."

"Then what else?"

"Tom and you and me all have friends. I figure now's the time to find out what kind of friends they are."

"The bucks that have the women and Tom's boy will have joined a bigger village by this time."

"Probably. And there's another hitch. We may not be able to get enough men together to do any good."

"What if we can't?"

"We can try to hire some. If that don't work, then the Army is all that's left. Maybe they could be talked into mounting a campaign against the Indians."

"You mean you'd enlist to go along?"

"Damn right I would. If I couldn't get on as scout."

Frank Denton nodded. "Wait till I get dressed and I'll go with you."

Clay gulped the last of the foul-tasting coffee. At least he was no longer alone. He didn't know Frank Denton very well, but Frank was strong and tough and he was Tom's brother and had a personal stake in this, just as did Clay himself.

CHAPTER
SIX

Most of Clay's friends, like himself, had ranches which were scattered out across the thousands of square miles in the vicinity of Dodge. There were a few in town, of course. Clay did all his trading here. So had Tom Denton.

It was eight o'clock when Clay and Frank left the house and headed toward the center of town. Now that he was faced with the task of finding friends who would be willing to drop everything and ride south with him into a land teeming with hostiles, Clay's small doubts began to grow. Friendship is a fine and wonderful thing, but it is also fragile. Demands made upon it weaken it. It thrives only on generosity.

Every step Clay took increased his doubts. After all, these friends he had in Dodge City owed nothing to him. Their relations had been of a business nature. He had bought what he needed from them and had paid for what he got. They owed him no more than he owed them. Would he, for example, have mortgaged his ranch to help one of them in a financial crisis?

He swore to himself and Frank Denton glanced at him curiously. "What's the matter with you?"

Clay shook his head. "Nothing. Who shall we see first?"

"Linkmeier, the gunsmith. He and Tom were close as hell. Their families used to get together every time Tom was in town."

Clay nodded. He knew Linkmeier, liked him and trusted him. He'd brought two guns to him to be repaired, and had bought two new ones from him. The two headed straight up the street toward Linkmeier's shop.

A bell tinkled as they went in and Silas Linkmeier came from the rear, a leather apron like one worn by blacksmiths on, and a revolver cylinder in his hands. He grinned when he saw who his visitors were. "Hello Frank. Hello Clay. Where's Tom? Didn't you bring him along?"

Clay didn't see any reason for beating around the bush. He said, "Tom's dead, Silas. His wife and boy have been kidnapped by the Cheyennes along with Julia."

"Oh Christ! You can't mean it!"

Clay said, "I mean it."

"What are you going to do?" There was genuine concern on Linkmeier's face.

Clay said, "Tom and me tracked them, naturally, as soon as we made sure they weren't in the ashes of the burned-out house. Followed 'em for a week or more and finally caught up with them. Tom was to get their horses on one side of camp and I was to get the women and Tom's kid out on the other when the bucks ran after their ponies. Trouble was, Tom ran into trouble.

52

He had to shoot and the whole camp was aroused. I couldn't get to the women and I had to run. Tom got away with their ponies but he took a slug while he was doing it. Anyways, I got him before the Indians could. I gave him a decent burial."

Linkmeier was shaking his head. "That's terrible! Terrible! Have you talked to the commandant out at Fort Dodge?"

Clay said, "He's the last resort. If the Army goes charging down there, the Indians will kill the women and Tom's boy before they get a chance to rescue them. You know how those damned redskins hate to get caught with any white prisoners."

"What can you do now, then?"

Frank broke in. "That's why we're here. We figure if we can get about twenty of our friends together, armed with shotguns, revolvers, and Spencers, that we can go down there and save the women's lives. Frankie's too."

Clay was watching Linkmeier's face carefully. He saw the change in it, the change from compassion and sympathy to reluctance and doubt. His eyes met Clay's and he tried determinedly to hold Clay's glance. He failed and looked away. Clay knew, then, even though it had not yet been given, what his answer was going to be.

Linkmeier said, "Hell, boys, you know how much I think of you. You know how much the wife and me thought — think of Tom's wife and boy. Hell, every time Tom brought his family to town, we'd all get together and have a picnic or something. But you're talking about something that might take weeks. Or even months. I got a mortgage on this shop and on my house. If I close up and go away, a new man'll start up for sure. There's Sam Dilly, out at Circle 8, who'd love to have the gun business I got now. He'd quit the job out there and open up a shop in town and by the time I got back, he'd have it all because he's as good a gunsmith as I am. Gettin' up in years, though, and he can't do ranch work many winters and that's for sure."

Frank Denton's face had hardened, closed around his narrowed eyes. He said, with no warmth left in his voice, "Hire him. Get him here to do your work for you."

Linkmeier shook his head. "I'd just be providing him with a shop. Maybe when I came back he'd turn the shop back to me, but by then he'd have the business."

Denton's voice now was cold, with anger churning in its depths. "Don't think much of yourself, do you?"

Linkmeier's face flushed painfully. He said with defensive anger, "It would likely cost me my shop, my house, and my business. I got to tell you plain, boys, I owe my wife more than I owe you boys."

Clay had expected something like this but it still hit him like a blow in the stomach. Not because they had lost Linkmeier's help, but because he was afraid they were going to get similar stories from all the others they asked.

Frank Denton was looking at Linkmeier as if he was going to hit him. Finally he looked at Clay. "I thought this sonofabitch was Tom's friend. I was wrong. Let's get the hell out of here."

54

Clay nodded. He felt sick with disappointment, but he was too fair a man to put all the blame on Linkmeier. He had to ask himself how quickly he himself might have charged off to help in what seemed an impossible task, knowing that doing so would probably cost him his livelihood.

The two went out, and Frank Denton paced furiously for a block before Clay could slow him down. Frank kept muttering, "The sonofabitch! The dirty sonofabitch!"

Clay waited until he had voiced all the fury that had built up in him. Then he said, "I know how you feel. I feel the same way. But you've got to look at it this way too. We're asking an awful lot. Weeks, maybe months. Fifteen or twenty men against the whole damned Cheyenne Nation."

Frank glared at him. "You sound like you're thinkin' of giving up."

Anger flared in Clay, but he fought it down. Evenly he said, "I'm not giving up. Not until we've got the women and Tom's boy back or until I'm dead. Don't you have any doubts about that."

"Then let's get to it. There are other friends of yours or Tom's or mine in town."

Clay didn't suggest that the story they'd get from the others might be the same as they'd gotten from Linkmeier. Frank was going to have to find that out for himself. He asked, "All right, who's next?"

"Jackson. I've bought plenty from him over the years I've been here."

Clay nodded. "Let's try him then." Jackson ran Jackson's Mercantile and Clay himself bought his supplies exclusively from him. He'd always considered Jackson a friend, but he was beginning to realize that there are numerous kinds of friends and few who will risk their lives for you, or give up their livelihood, or even donate a few weeks or months to their friendship with you. It was a sobering and disillusioning thing for him to realize and it depressed him. But he told himself that he might be wrong. With Jackson it might be different. Or even if it wasn't, the friends he had on ranches scattered around Dodge would certainly look at things differently.

They strode swiftly up the street to Jackson's Mercantile. Jackson was sweeping the boardwalk in front. He glanced up. Frank hesitated, so Clay said, "My ranch was attacked by Cheyennes a couple of weeks ago. Tom's wife and boy and Julia were all together there and the Cheyennes took them. Tom and me went after them, but Tom got killed. Now I need some help from my friends to go after them again."

The look of refusal came more quickly to Jackson's face. He was a scrawny man with a clipped mustache. He said briskly, "Can't leave the store, boys, you know that. Go broke if I did."

"Can't you get someone . . . ? I'd pay his wages and be glad to do it."

But Jackson was already shaking his head.

Frank Denton's face was beet red. He said, "You dirty bastard!"

56

Clay caught his arm. "No use, Frank. Let's get horses and ride out to see if some of Tom's and my ranch friends won't help."

"Those bastards will give us the same story."

"Maybe not. It's worth a day's time to try, isn't it?"

Denton nodded grudgingly. He looked straight at Jackson. "You sonofabitch!"

Jackson was angry too by now. He said, "I'm in business. I'm not an Indian fighter. Go to the people who are, the Army. Let them get your women back for you."

Clay and Frank strode away. Clay guided Frank, who was nearly blind with fury, toward the livery barn. Frank kept muttering, "The bastards! Hell, a man sure finds out how many friends he's got when he calls on 'em for help."

Clay didn't say anything, but he was pretty sure they were going to get the same kind of response out of the ranchers they visited. The ranchers would be afraid to leave their own families while the Indian scare was on. Or they wouldn't be able to leave their work. There would be all kinds of excuses, but what the final answer would be was no. Go to the Army. Do it yourself. Or hire some of the hardcases that hung around Dodge all the time.

They got their horses at the livery stable, mounted, and rode out of town. Clay Holley caught himself heading toward home without even thinking about it. Then he thought about Julia and Sally Denton and the boy. He thought of them still in the hands of the

Indians. And suddenly his apparent helplessness infuriated him as much as it already had Frank Denton.

He took a fork in the road about a quarter mile from town and headed for Del Hanley's place. Living less than a mile from town, Del shouldn't be afraid of Indians attacking his place.

They reached it shortly. There was a two-story house, painted white. There was a big red barn behind the house, and numerous other buildings. Del came out of the barn and stood with hands on hips watching them ride in.

Clay glanced at Frank. Frank's face was still red, his eyes still angry. Clay said, "Let me do the talking, Frank. The way you're feeling, you'll raise hell with him before he had a chance to say yes *or* no."

Frank turned his head and glared. Finally the faintest of rueful smiles touched his face. "It just makes me so goddam mad . . ."

Clay said, "I guess a man shouldn't ever ask anything of his friends. That way he never finds out one way or the other what kind of friends they are."

They reached Del, and Clay swung to the ground. Frank stayed on his horse, as if convinced this wasn't even worth dismounting for. Clay said, "I don't know whether you heard or not, but Cheyennes hit my place about two weeks ago. Tom Denton's wife and boy were there with Julia. They took both women and Frankie and burned the house."

Del whistled, but Clay could already see a certain wariness coming into his eyes. He said, "That's terrible! I'm sorry."

Clay went on, "Tom and me went after them. Caught up with them too. But things went wrong. I was going in to get the women away while Tom ran the horses off. Trouble was, Tom had to shoot. After that we never had a chance. Tom got shot and died."

Del started to say something, but Frank Denton didn't give him a chance. He said, "We're asking our friends to help. We need to get up twenty or twenty-five men. With that many armed with Spencers, revolvers, and shotguns, I figure we can get those women and Frankie back."

The wariness was stronger in Del. He looked as if he'd like to get away. Frank started to say something intemperate, but Clay cut him off. "Put yourself in our place, Del. Think what it would be like if it was your wife and son." He was begging now, but almost immediately he knew it wasn't going to do any good.

Del said, "I'd like to help you, boys, but if I leave here it might be my wife and son those red devils get next. Since them Cheyennes have been raisin' hell, I haven't been getting more than a couple of hundred yards from the house. Except when we go to town and then I take Mary and Jimmy along."

Clay discarded all his pride. He said, "Please, Del. For God's sake, help us out!"

"How many more you got?"

"Not any yet." Clay hated to say it. He felt Frank's glare on him and knew Frank would have lied.

Del said, with relief apparent in his voice, "Well, I'll tell you what. You get twenty besides yourselves and I'll go along. I'll take Mary and Jimmy to town and leave them there."

There was nothing more to say. Frank and Clay stared at Del for several moments until Del lowered his glance and said, "Well, I got work to do."

Frank tried one more time. "Just how the hell do you think we're going to get twenty if all of them give us the same stinking answer you did?"

But Del had his back turned and did not reply.

Frank started muttering as they rode away. Clay felt a little sick at his stomach. He had honestly believed he could count on most of the many friends he had made here over the years. Now he knew that even if he found a few who would help, it wasn't going to be enough. Most were going to give him and Frank the same answers that the others had.

He thought, My God, what can I do now?

CHAPTER
SEVEN

The two men rode along in silence for a long time until they reached the fork in the road. Here both stopped. Frank looked at Clay, his fury still smoldering.

Clay said, "We can go see some more people, but I don't think it will do any good. And it's going to take a lot of time. The people you know and those Tom and I know are scattered over hundreds of square miles."

"So what else can we do?"

"We can go to Fort Dodge. Hell, the reason the Army's here is to protect the people who live out here. Maybe the commandant out there will give us a troop of cavalry."

"Not likely." Frank was sour and angry and thoroughly discouraged. Clay felt the same way except that it probably didn't show as much. It was a shock to discover that the men you thought were good and solid friends were only fair-weather friends.

Finally Frank shrugged. "Can't hurt, I guess. Besides, the only other thing we can do is go after them ourselves. And the chance of pulling that off is practically zero. We'd only get the women killed."

Clay said, "That's a chance even if the Army helps. You've got to realize it." He stared at Frank Denton's face, seeing an expression there that revealed something he had never suspected and that Denton probably had never, even unconsciously, betrayed to anybody else. Frank was in love with Sally, who had been his brother's wife. Clay quickly looked away, for fear his own expression might reveal what he had guessed.

Clay reined his horse around and headed along the road that led to Fort Dodge. Frank fell in behind. Once Clay glanced around and caught Frank watching him closely as if he knew that Clay had somehow guessed the secret he had tried so long to hide.

Half a mile farther on, Frank said, "That sonofabitch will never help us."

"We don't know that yet."

Frank said, "Hell, the damned Indians have been coming up to within yelling distance of the fort all summer and the Army hasn't been able to do anything. What makes you think they can do better now?"

Clay said patiently, "It's worth trying. Unless you've got a better idea."

"Well, it won't take long to find out."

They rode at a steady trot and finally brought the sprawling buildings and scrubby trees of the fort into sight. There was a troop of infantry on the parade, marching back and forth to the commands of their sergeant while a lieutenant stood off to one side and watched.

A soldier intercepted the two and asked who they wanted to see. Clay said, "The commandant. General Sully."

The soldier looked doubtful, but he asked, "Who shall I say . . . ?"

"Clay Holley and Frank Denton. You tell him it's about two white women and a boy that have been kidnapped by the Indians."

"Yes, sir. You come this way." The soldier led them across the corner of the parade, past regimental headquarters to Sully's quarters, the finest looking house on officers' row. They dismounted and tied their horses, while the soldier went up onto the porch and knocked on the door.

The door opened slightly and the soldier spoke to whoever had answered it. A few moments later the door opened wide and Sully, in full uniform, asked them to come in. The soldier departed reluctantly, plainly curious and wishing he could hear what was going on.

Sully escorted them into a small room off the parlor where there were several comfortable chairs, a desk, and some shelves filled with books. "The private tells me you said something about two kidnapped women and a boy."

Clay nodded, resisting the impulse to call Sully "sir." He had been a lieutenant in the war, and calling generals "sir" just came naturally. Sully looked interested and concerned as Clay related the story of the raid and their failure to rescue the women. "There wasn't anything I could do. I'd just have got myself killed, and that wouldn't have helped my wife."

"What about Tom? Did he run the horses off?"

Clay nodded. "Got himself shot, though, doing it. I buried him and came back to Dodge to see if I couldn't get some help."

"It's illegal for civilians to mount an expedition against the Indians."

Clay felt irritation touch him. He felt like saying, "To hell with legality." But he didn't. He only said, "I couldn't get any of my friends or Frank's to help. They've all got excuses . . ."

"So you want help from me?"

Clay said, "Yes, sir. We figure a troop of cavalry, with Frank and me to scout. I can take 'em straight to the place we last saw those Indians. Between Frank and me we can trail them to wherever they went from there."

"Do you have the slightest idea how many Indians there are within a hundred miles of this fort?"

Clay shook his head. "To tell you the truth, General, I don't much care. All I care about is the few that have my wife and Tom Denton's wife and boy."

"I can't go chasing off . . ."

Clay interrupted. "General, what's the Army out here for?"

Sully had the grace to look embarrassed. "To keep order. To protect the citizens from the Indians."

"That's all I'm asking you to do. I don't even want your whole command, so you can't say your fort will be left without an adequate defense."

Sully stared at the pair for a moment. "This isn't generally known, gentlemen, and I don't want it known. But preparations are underway for a major campaign against the Cheyennes. We're going to teach those red devils a lesson they're not likely to soon forget. I just can't spare a troop, and even if I could, I wouldn't want to stir the Indians up by embarking on a diversionary campaign such as you suggest."

It took an instant for that to soak in. A major campaign against the Indians was good news in one way, hellish bad news in another. But to call the rescue of two white women and a little boy a "diversionary campaign" . . .

Clay said, "General, I don't want to quarrel with you. But do you realize what will happen to those two women and that little boy if you make a full-scale attack against the camp where they're being held?"

Sully shrugged faintly. "The fortunes of war, gentlemen. I can't help what the Indians do to their captives when they're attacked."

"What you call a 'diversionary attack' might save their lives."

Sully had a stubborn look on his face now. He was shaking his head. "I can't help you, gentlemen. I'm in command of this post, but I still get my orders from higher up."

Frank Denton was on his feet. His face was florid, his eyes blazing. He said, "You stupid sonofabitch . . ." He took a step toward Sully, as if he meant to go around the desk.

Sully bawled, "Orderly! Orderly!"

But Clay had hold of Denton's arm. He said, "Frank, it's no use. Come on."

He literally dragged Frank Denton from the office. The orderly came in as they went out, and Sully said angrily, "See that those two civilians leave the post immediately!"

Clay untied his horse and Frank followed suit. They mounted and headed back toward Dodge. When they were out of earshot of Sully and the orderly, Clay said angrily, "When are you ever going to learn to keep your damned mouth shut?"

Frank had the grace to look ashamed but he did not reply. The two rode back to Dodge City, silent most of the way. They went to the hotel and ate.

As they were finishing, Frank said, "No use you staying at the hotel. There's an extra bed at my place you can use."

Clay nodded. He was going to be working closely with Frank Denton from now on and he'd just as well know what Frank was doing if he could. Denton's temper had already caused trouble and it might cause more.

Finished with eating, he went upstairs and got his things out of his room. He turned his key in at the desk, paid his bill, then followed Frank outside. They put up their horses at the livery stable and walked the short distance to Frank Denton's house.

Clay, exhausted from trying hard to get help today and failing so miserably, went right to bed. But it was a long time before he went to sleep. Having failed to get his friends to help and having failed to get any co-operation from the Army, tomorrow he would try all that he had left. He'd raise what money he could on his cattle and his ranch and try to hire an army or hardcases from among those who regularly hung around the saloons in Dodge.

CHAPTER
EIGHT

Clay Holley left Frank Denton's place as soon as he thought the bank would be open, but he still had to wait twenty minutes in front of it before the teller arrived. Clay had an account in the bank, so he was recognized immediately. The teller greeted him. "Good morning, Mr. Holley. Come right on in."

"I want to see Mr. Cordrey."

"He won't be in for half an hour or so. Can I help?"

Holley shook his head. "I need to borrow money on my ranch and cattle."

The teller looked puzzled, but he ushered Clay back to Ben Cordrey's office and Clay sat down to wait.

It was a dark office, with somber, dark furniture, a black potbellied stove in one corner and a huge iron safe with gold lettering on its front in the other. Clay found himself rehearsing what he was going to say, and angrily made himself stop. There was no call for nervousness or doubt. He owned two sections of good grassland and leased several more. He put up a couple of hundred tons of hay a year. He had five hundred cattle, more or less.

Cordrey arrived half an hour after the teller had opened the bank. He came back to his office, red-faced, smiling. "Smell of fall in the air this morning, Mr. Holley. Won't be long and we'll be up to our knees in snow. Have a good hay crop this year?"

Holly nodded, stood up, and shook Cordrey's hand. "About the usual. Enough to get us through the winter comfortably."

Cordrey hung his hat up and sat down behind his desk. "How's Mrs. Holley?"

"That's why I'm here. While Tom Denton and I were gathering and shipping those two- and three-year-olds, Indians attacked my place. Burned the house and kidnapped my wife and Tom's and Tom's little boy."

Shock showed in Cordrey's eyes. "That's terrible! That's absolutely terrible!"

"Tom and I went after them. There were nine to start but by the time we caught up, there were more than that. We talked it over and decided one of us was to run off their horse herd while the other tried to get the women and Frankie away. Tom chose to run the horse herd off, but he must have run into trouble because he had to shoot. That woke the whole camp up and I never had a chance to get near the women. Not only that, Tom got shot in the chest. He died and I buried him down there."

"I'm awfully sorry, Mr. Holley. I really am. What . . . ?"

"Well, I've thought of nothing else since it happened. If I try going to the Indian agent, the Cheyennes will probably kill both women and Frankie before they'll admit to having them. I tried to get the Army to go after the Indians, but they're planning an expedition against them and they won't help. I've tried getting friends without any more success. That leaves an expedition of hardcases and it's going to take money to hire them."

"And you need to borrow it?"

"Yes."

"How much . . . do you have any idea how much it's going to take?"

Clay thought about that, realizing he should have considered it earlier. Finally he said, "Well, I don't see how any less than forty of that kind of men would have a chance. The nine who attacked my place were joined by at least that many more and the chances are that they all ended up in some village where there were even more."

"How much will you have to pay each of those forty men?"

Clay shrugged. "I can't see good men risking as much as they'll be risking for less than a couple of hundred each, particularly if they furnish their own horses and guns. That comes to eight thousand dollars. Maybe a couple of thousand more in expenses. Ten thousand dollars, I guess."

Cordrey was silent a long time. Finally he asked, "How many cattle do you have?"

"Five, maybe six hundred head."

"At ten dollars a head, which is a pretty good price considering that a lot of them are cows, calves, and yearlings, that's only half of ten thousand. And the bank simply can't loan more than half their value at the most. I'm afraid twenty-five hundred would be the best that I could do."

"I've got two sections of land."

Cordrey shook his head. "With the country overrun with Indians, land is too risky to use as security for a loan."

Clay Holley felt anger stir in him. Cordrey was detached, businesslike. Gone was his original shock and sympathy over the kidnapping of the two women and the small son of Tom Denton.

He asked coldly, "How much?"

"Twenty-five hundred. I'm sorry, Mr. Holley. I want to help, but I have our stockholders to think about. And I'd have to send some man out to tally your cattle before I could go that far."

"You won't take my word?"

Cordrey's eyes got a little colder. "I can't take anybody's word, Mr. Holley. I'd have to have a tally of the cattle before I could do a thing."

"That would take a couple of weeks."

"At least. But if your wife and Mrs. Denton are still alive, the chances are they won't be killed at this late date."

Clay Holley clenched his fists. He wanted to lash out at Cordrey, to relieve his anger in words. He fought to restrain himself. He wasn't going to close any doors just to satisfy his own anger.

He asked, "What about Tom Denton's place? His brother could sign the note."

Cordrey shook his head. "He doesn't own the place, Mr. Holley. Mrs. Denton does. Until we know she and her son are dead . . ."

Holley got to his feet. He did not extend his hand. He said, fighting to keep his fury out of his voice, "I'll let you know."

"Yes. Mr. Holley. I hope you won't be too disturbed. This is a business and it has to be run in a businesslike way. We have to have security."

"And a man's character isn't security?" Holley couldn't resist saying that.

"Of course it is. If I didn't know you, I'd have said no right away."

Holley nodded and walked up the long aisle to the front of the bank. Twenty-five hundred dollars wasn't going to be nearly enough. Not even with what he had in the bank. But he'd try. He had to try. He met Frank Denton coming up the street. "What did he say?"

"He said twenty-five hundred on my place and nothing on Tom's."

"Not even if I sign the note?"

"He says you can't sign. Not until it's sure Sally and Frankie are dead."

"Well, by God, I'll see about that!" Frank Denton started away, heading toward the bank.

Clay caught up and seized Denton's arm. "It won't do any good. It will only make things worse and we might need the twenty-five hundred."

For an instant, he thought he was going to have to fight Denton to keep him away from the bank. He could see the fury in Denton's eyes, fury that matched that which he'd felt when Cordrey refused him earlier. And he could see something else, blame for what had happened to Tom, blame that he hadn't been able to save Tom's wife and son from the Indians, blame because Tom was dead and he was not.

He repeated, "It won't do any good."

The two stood there for a long time, glaring into each other's eyes. Finally Frank Denton relaxed. "I guess you're right. Considering what a cold-blooded sonofabitch that Cordrey is."

Clay made no defense of the banker. He said, "Next best thing is to try and sell. Let's go down to the corrals and see what we can do. If I could get ten dollars a head for the cattle, or twelve, maybe it would be enough."

"They'd have to be gathered and tallied."

Clay admitted that he was right. He came to terms with something else. He wasn't going to be able to ride south with a rescue party in the next week or ten days. It was going to take time. If he sold the cattle, they'd have to be rounded up. Men would have to be hired for that task, and hiring men to go out, singly and in pairs, to gather cattle where hostiles were known to be roaming would in itself be no easy task. And if he borrowed on the cattle, they would have to be tallied, if not gathered. That also would take time and part of the money he hoped to borrow on them. Furthermore, a tally would necessarily be less thorough than a roundup would be. He might be able to tally no more than half to two thirds of the cattle he actually owned. Indians might have scattered them, might even have slaughtered some for sport if not for food.

Even at this hour of the morning, the corrals that stretched for half a mile along the railroad tracks were busy. A trainload of cattle cars clanked slowly into place, positioning the first car in front of a loading chute. Yelling men on horses crowded cattle up the loading chute into the car.

Clay spotted Chuck McGrath, the buyer to whom he had sold his two- and three-year-olds, sitting on the top rail of the corral. He climbed up beside McGrath. "I've got to talk to you."

"Later. These are mine and I want to make sure they get loaded right."

Frank Denton gripped McGrath's arm. His face was hard. He said, "Now. Listen to what he's got to say."

Anger flared briefly in McGrath's eyes, then went away. He yelled at one of the men crowding the cattle up the chute. "Take over. I'll be right back." He jumped down from the corral and followed Frank Denton and Clay along the alleyway until they were out of the dust and noise of the bawling beasts. He said, "All right, but make it quick."

Clay said, "Cheyennes attacked and burned my house and stole my wife and Tom Denton's wife and boy. We went after them but we couldn't get them back and Tom Denton was killed. Now I've got to hire some men and go after them again. To hire men I need money and what I got for my two- and three-year-olds isn't near enough. I've got to sell the rest of my cattle and I've got to sell them right away."

McGrath said, "I'm sorry. I really am. About what happened to your wife and Tom's. Are they still alive? You're sure?"

"They were alive when we tried to get them away."

"Whereabouts was that?"

"South of here by about a week."

"You're sure they were Cheyennes? If they went down there, they could have been Comanch."

"No. I'm not sure. But I think they were Cheyennes. They were taller than Comanch."

"You can't go down there without forty or fifty men."

"I know."

"And you couldn't hire men to ride that deep into Indian country for less than a couple of hundred each. That's close to ten thousand bucks. How many cattle you got left?"

"Five, maybe six hundred, counting calves."

"That's not enough."

"My ranch. Two sections of land."

McGrath was already regretfully shaking his head. "I haven't got ten thousand dollars to tie up right now. Cattle are coming in every day. I've got to be able to buy them when they do come in or I'm out of business."

Clay asked, "What about the bank? Can't *you* borrow . . . ?"

"Have you been up and talked to that sonofabitch?"

Clay nodded.

"Then you know what I'm up against. I've already borrowed every cent he'll let me have. If I use part of it to loan to you, he'll blow sky high. I'm sorry, Clay. I know how you feel and I'd like to help, but I've got my tail in a crack. Have you been out to Fort Dodge to see the commandant?"

Numbly Clay nodded his head. He could raise twenty-five hundred at the bank and he had another fifteen hundred left from the money he'd gotten for his two- and three-year-olds. That would hire no more than fifteen to twenty men and that few men wouldn't consider riding south into country where there were hundreds, maybe thousands of hostiles. Not for money anyway.

He felt the bitter taste of defeat as he turned away. Frank Denton was glaring at McGrath as if he was going to start a fight. Clay grabbed his arm. "That won't do any good."

"There are other buyers. McGrath ain't the only one."

"We'll try them then. But if we can't get enough to hire at least forty men, there's no use trying to get anyone to go. And there's no way we're going to raise enough money for forty men."

Frank Denton stood there scowling for several moments. Finally he shrugged. "I'll go home and get some things. Then I'll come down after my horse."

Clay Holley said, "I'll meet you there." He headed along the alleyway between the crowded corrals toward the lower end of the street where the livery stable was. A bleak feeling of defeat was creeping over him. He'd go on trying until he had exhausted every chance of mounting an expedition against the Indians. He'd talk to every cattle and land buyer in town. He'd see every moneylender before he would give up. And finally, if there was no other way, he and Frank Denton would have to ride south alone. Better to die trying than not to try at all.

CHAPTER
NINE

The next two days were the most frustrating and defeating that Clay Holley had ever experienced. He talked to cattle buyer after cattle buyer. He talked with land speculator after land speculator. He got offers, naturally, but none of them were even close.

He also talked with the men who frequented the saloons, the men who had come up the trail from Texas with the cattle herds, those who lived off them and the drifters that came and stayed for a week or two and then moved on. They wanted more than he could pay. The buyers and lenders offered less than he had to have. Nor was the gap a narrow one. No matter how he tried, he couldn't raise even half the money it would take to hire and outfit an expedition to go south into Indian country to rescue his wife and the wife and son of Tom Denton.

On the third day, he was sitting in one of the saloons when a group of soldiers from Fort Dodge came in. Frank Denton was with him and both were morose, edgy, and feeling quarrelsome.

Clay heard the name General Sully mentioned. He also heard the soldiers talking about the coming expedition that Sully had mentioned to them a couple of days before.

It suddenly occurred to Clay that this was the only chance he and Frank had left, short of riding south alone. If Sully's expedition was heading south, maybe they could figure out some way of going along.

Frank seemed to have had the same idea at the same time. The two left their table immediately and headed for the one where the soldiers were. As Clay crossed the room, he beckoned to the bartender. "Bring a bottle for the soldiers."

He waited until the bartender had arrived at the table with the bottle and glasses, bringing the news that he had bought the drinks. The soldiers glanced up at him agreeably and he said, "Couldn't help overhearing you mention the campaign General Sully is planning. You boys have any idea which way he's going to go?"

One of the soldiers, redheaded, skinny, and no more than nineteen, said, "He'd have to go south if he wanted to find any Indians, wouldn't he? That's where they head long before the weather starts gettin' cold. And the ducks and geese are already heading south."

Clay said, "Maybe he don't want to find any Indians."

"Not the general, mister. He'll go where the Indians are."

"When you leaving?"

"Three days. September first."

Clay pulled out a chair and told the three soldiers about Julia and Sally Denton and her boy. He said, "If you go south, I want to go along. So does Frank here. He's the boy's uncle."

The redheaded soldier shrugged sympathetically. "I'd like to tell you that you could. But the general won't let no civilians go along." His face brightened suddenly. "Not unless you was to sign on as scouts."

Clay was thinking about the cursing Frank had given Sully as they left. Now he asked, "Who's in charge of scouts?"

"Captain Jamieson. Let's see, he's officer of the day today. He ought to be at headquarters. Know where that is?"

Clay nodded. He looked at Frank, then crossed to the bar. He paid for the first bottle and added enough for a second. To Frank he said, "Let's go."

Frank followed him out of the saloon. They got their horses and rode out of town, heading for Fort Dodge. If they could see Jamieson without first seeing Sully, then maybe they could get on as scouts. If not and if the expedition really was going south, then they could enlist, even if they had to sign up as privates.

Frank had been a sergeant during the war and Clay had been a lieutenant of cavalry but it wasn't likely they'd get ranks close to those.

They were almost to the door leading to headquarters when Sully came unexpectedly out of his quarters. He glared at them. "What the hell are you two doing here?"

For once, Frank was speechless. Clay said, "We'd like to offer our services as scouts, General. Both of us know the country south of here like we know the backs of our hands."

Sully stared at Denton incredulously. "You curse me and then you have the gall to come out here and ask for a job as scout? Well, by God, the answer is no. And if you're both not off the post in five minutes, I'll have you escorted off!"

Behind Clay and Frank, a captain had heard the angry talk and had come out of headquarters. "Trouble, General?"

"Nothing I can't handle. These two tried to sign on as scouts. But they're leaving. Right away." He turned and disappeared into his quarters.

Captain Jamieson grinned faintly. "You sure managed to get him riled."

Clay said, "Frank here cussed him out a couple of days ago." He headed along the street in front of the buildings, leading his horse.

The captain, curious, kept pace and Frank brought up the rear. Jamieson seemed genuinely interested, so Clay told him the whole story of his wife's kidnapping, of his attempts to rescue her, of his recent attempts to get help. Now, he said, he understood the Army was going after the Indians on September 1. If they were going south, he said, he'd like to go along.

Jamieson confided a bit ruefully that Sully hadn't discussed his plans with anyone, but that since the Cheyennes were mostly south of Fort Dodge at this time of year, it made sense that they'd go in that direction. And he made an offer, after querying them about their previous military service, that if they wanted to sign on as privates, they could. He said they were short of men and that Sully would cool off, given time, because he always did.

Clay looked at Frank. He had tried everything he could think of to rescue Julia and Sally and her boy. There was no assurance, of course, that Sully would take his troops south or that, even if he did, he would make contact with the Cheyennes who had taken the women and boy prisoners.

Frank's expression told Clay he was thinking along the same desperate lines. Frank nodded faintly.

Two hours later they were sworn in, both as privates. Immediately afterward, they were directed to the quartermaster's stores, where they were outfitted with uniforms. Later, each was issued a horse, a McClellan saddle, a bridle, saddle blanket, bedroll, and mess kit. Each was given a Spencer rifle and fifty rounds of ammunition and was assigned to a barracks. Both were assigned to G Troop of the 7th Cavalry.

The day was August 29. The two were allowed the rest of the day to return their horses to Dodge City and to get rid of their civilian clothing and personal effects. They returned in the evening, uniformed now, committed to whatever the Army ordered them to do.

Clay admitted it was very doubtful if Sully's expedition would get anywhere near the village where his wife and Sally Denton were being held. But he also admitted that he had no other choice. There were hundreds, maybe thousands of hostile Cheyennes, Kiowas, and Comanches within a hundred miles. Only the Army had a chance of success against that many

Indians. He would just have to hope that General Sully headed south as everyone expected.

He and Frank had signed up for three years, but desertions were commonplace and deserters were rarely pursued, almost never caught. If the Army couldn't help him to find and rescue his wife, he could always desert and try to find some other way.

Neither man was a stranger to Army life. Except for the fact they had new uniforms, neither man stood out from the hundreds of other soldiers at the fort. The next two days were busy ones as a supply train was organized and outfitted, as each trooper readied his mount, had him shod, and checked his gear. Finally, early on the morning of September 1, the command departed from Fort Dodge.

Now, belatedly, Holley found out where the command was headed — for the confluence of the north and south branches of the Solomon River. Cheyennes had raided some small settlements there. Sully, with eleven troops of the 7th Cavalry under Major Elliott and a few companies of the 3rd Infantry, were to find and punish them.

The Solomon was almost as far north as Holley and Frank Denton wanted to go south. As the command rode north, Holley searched the column of twos behind him, looking almost frantically for Frank Denton's face. If Frank agreed, they would desert tonight. Again, the terrible feeling of defeat and frustration came over him. There had been, at least, a one-in-four chance that the column would head south. Instead they were heading north.

Glumly he rode, swallowing the dust of those ahead of him. General Sully rode in an ambulance at the head of the supply train with a few members of his staff. Young Major Elliott rode at the column's head.

Again and again Holley went back over the things he had done, over each move he had made. He could think of no stone he had left unturned. It had simply been impossible for him to do what he had tried to do.

Maybe, he thought, this expedition, even though it was headed north, would accomplish something. If they could defeat the Indians they encountered, others might go to their reservations, fearing a similar reprisal from the troops. Maybe deserting now would be the wrong thing to do.

He thought again of Julia, in the Indians' hands. And the almost uncontrollable feeling of impatience once more took hold of him. Yet he told himself that, like it or not, he was going to have to be patient. Sooner or later the Army would march south. Sooner or later he would get close to the camp where his wife was being held. Being patient might be the hardest thing he had ever done, but there was no other way.

Scarcely had they left Fort Dodge before Indians began to appear on the skylines ahead and on both sides of them. The Indians waved, and made obscene gestures whenever they were close enough for their gestures to be seen and understood.

Grumbling began among the men, and increased as time went on. Scarcely had light faded from the sky at their first night's camp before a band of warriors scattered the horses and mules of the wagon train, firing their guns into the air, screeching like maniacs. Sully ordered G Troop to pursue, but by the time the horses were saddled and the troop ready to ride, the Indians had disappeared. G Troop rode out nevertheless.

Less than half a mile from the bivouac derisive shouts from the Indians began to bombard them from all sides. Major Elliott, leading the troop, turned them in the direction from which the greatest volume of shouting appeared to be coming. They rode through the darkness for half an hour, seeing nothing, hearing only the continuing derisive shouts of the Indians. Once a bugle blew retreat. Sometimes obscenities in English were hurled at them from what seemed less than a hundred yards.

At last Elliott ordered them to reverse their direction and return to camp. They did, and the contemptuous shouts of the Indians followed them all the way.

Clay Holley and Frank Denton, along with the others, unsaddled and secured their horses on the G Troop picket line.

Denton said, "I think we made a mistake. Those sonsabitches ain't one damn bit scared of the Army. They're going to let us chase all over the country while they lay back and poke fun at us."

Glumly Clay said, "Looks like it."

"So what are we going to do?"

Clay Holley felt irritation touch his thoughts. He said, "Suppose you tell me. I've done everything I can think of. It's a cinch you and I can't go into Indian country alone and expect to accomplish anything, and we can't raise the money for enough men to do any good."

"This sure as hell ain't doing any good."

Angrily Holley stared at him. "Then quit. Desert. Give up. Let your brother's wife and son stay with the Indians. Who knows, maybe they'll get to like it if you leave them with the Indians long enough."

Frank said, "Damn you . . ."

"Well, what the hell do you expect me to say? We haven't got any control over what the Army does. We knew that when we joined."

"Then why did we join the goddam Army?"

"Because there was a chance. And there wasn't *any* chance sitting there in the saloon in Dodge."

Denton grumbled, but he made no more protests. Both men wrapped themselves in their blankets and lay down to sleep. They could still hear distant whoops and derisive yelling by the Indians that surrounded the bivouac. The supply train horses and mules, having been recovered, were now between the wagons and the camp under heavy guard.

The following morning Sully — usually called by his wartime brevet rank of brigadier general, but now a lieutenant colonel of infantry — suddenly gave up the idea of taking his command all the way to the Solomon River. Probably he knew that the Indians who had attacked the settlements there would be long gone by the time he and his command arrived.

Instead he headed south on a course that would bypass Fort Dodge by thirty or forty miles. Not privy to command decisions, neither Clay nor Frank Denton could know why he reversed direction the way he did. Perhaps his scouts advised it. Perhaps it was just a whim, or the certainty that he would find no Indians at the Solomon.

The change of direction did much to improve the mood of both Holley and Denton, however. Neither had much hope the command would encounter the village where Julia, Sally, and little Frankie were being held. But there was a chance, and there was no chance going north.

For three days they toiled south. Both the supply column and the infantry slowed them down. And always, on all sides, were the Indians, contemptuous, unafraid.

Sully stayed in his ambulance, directing the column from there. Rarely was he seen by his troops. Never did he march or ride with them.

There had been a certain excitement in the men when they rode out of Fort Dodge. Now it was gone. The men were sullen, apathetic, and morose. Morale was lower than Clay Holley had ever seen it in any unit during the war. Fights were frequent. The troopers seemed to want to take out their frustration over the Indians' taunts on each other.

Finally the last straw was reached, as a score of screeching Indians rode out of a dry wash the column had just crossed. They cut two troopers off the rear guard, clubbed them, and caught them as they fell from their mounts. Leading the two captured cavalry mounts and dragging the two unconscious troopers, the Indians galloped away.

86

So sudden and unexpected was the assault, so devastating was its success, that it was several minutes before the lieutenant commanding the rear guard was even notified. By the time he had organized a pursuit, the Indians had disappeared.

And from Sully's ambulance came the word, "Return to the column at once. We are returning to the Fort."

The lieutenant and his rescue detachment reluctantly returned. The column moved out toward Fort Dodge, with its morale even lower now, as a result of the successful kidnapping of the two troopers from the rear guard.

From a practical standpoint, stopping the pursuit made sense, Holley admitted to himself. If the two kidnapped troopers weren't already dead, they would be before any rescue party got to them.

But there was another thing he knew Sully should have considered carefully before calling off the pursuit. The command had been taunted and mocked by the Indians ever since it left Fort Dodge. The kidnapping had been the ultimate display of the Indians' contempt.

Not to avenge dishonored every man in the command. It dishonored every soldier in every United States Army command everywhere.

Troopers and infantrymen traveled in glum silence, no longer even bothering to look toward the taunting Indians, except for those in the rear guard and those in exposed positions, who were considerably more vigilant than they had been before.

Holley remembered another wartime brevet general who had allowed men to be seized from the rear guard of his command, and who had not bothered to recover their bodies or try to rescue them.

The man's name was Custer. For that, and for a series of other offenses, he had been court-martialed and suspended from duty for a year.

Holley suddenly realized that Custer's suspension was almost up. And the 7th was Custer's regiment. He would be returning to it, but it was doubtful if he would do any better than General Sully had.

Except that it would be winter when Custer returned to his command. And maybe in the winter things would be different.

CHAPTER
TEN

It was a glum and defeated column that returned to Fort Dodge. Sully still rode in his ambulance, unseen by the men, apparently not wanting to come face to face with them. And their mood was quickly communicated to those who had remained at the fort, both soldiers and civilians. Major Elliott's terse report to the officer of the day was, "We engaged no hostiles. They apparently didn't want to fight."

Holley and Frank Denton took care of their mounts, unsaddling, currying, watering, and feeding them. With that done, they trudged toward the barracks, downcast and sour. Once, Frank growled, "You and your ideas!"

Holley opened his mouth to snap back at him, but closed it without saying anything. Joining the Army had not, it now appeared, been the best idea he'd ever had. And yet, going back over the alternatives in his mind, he knew there was nothing else they could have done.

The days dragged. There were no drills, so time lay heavily on the hands of the men. There were some old newspapers and a few dime novels around the barracks, nearly worn out by constant use.

Holley fumed at the inactivity even more than most of the other men. All he could think about was Julia in the hands of the Indians. Her child was due in early December and, unless she was rescued before then, she'd have to bear it alone, the way the Indians did. Still, he consoled himself, the Indian women seemed to have no trouble bearing children.

The thought that terrified him most of all was that, before he was able to rescue her, he himself might be killed. If that happened, Julia would remain with the Indians, gradually becoming one of them as her hope of rescue faded and finally died. His child would grow up as wild and savage as any true Indian.

In late September the newspapers reported that General Sheridan, in St. Louis, had issued a proclamation to the effect that a state of war existed between the United States and the Cheyennes and Arapahos. He suggested, furthermore, that since all Indians looked alike, those who were peaceably inclined should go at once to their reservations within the Indian Territory, south of the Kansas line. There they would be provided for by their agents.

A letter from General Sherman to Secretary of War Schofield was quoted in one of the papers to the effect that he had dispatched General Hazen to the frontier with a sum of money to aid the agents in providing food for the peaceful portions of the two tribes while en route to and after their arival at their new homes.

It was to be hoped, editorialized the paper's editor, that a substantial number of the hostiles now roaming the plains would take advantage of the opportunity, particularly since the winter was fast approaching. But, concluded the editorial, it was doubtful if they would until deep snows and bitter cold actually drove them there. Then, the writer suggested bitterly, all hostiles would suddenly become peacefully inclined. And so they would remain until spring weather brought new grass and new freedom for them again.

Rumors began circulating within the fort. The most prevalent one was that Custer, at General Sheridan's and Sully's request, had been reinstated as commander of the 7th Cavalry. He was even now on his way to take command of his regiment. It was also rumored that ten or eleven troops of the 7th would move on October 1 from Medicine Lodge Creek toward the Wichita Mountains.

Another rumor said that Custer had met with Sheridan at Fort Hays, that they had planned the strategy for the campaign.

Many of the rumors were wild and without basis in fact. Others were remarkably accurate, suggesting that they were based on solid information revealed by someone who knew. One of these was that a base camp would be established close to the border of the new Indian reservations. From this camp, a column of eleven troops of the 7th Cavalry and two or three of the 19th Kansas Volunteer Cavalry would proceed south against the Indians.

Sourly the disheartened troopers of the 7th Cavalry discussed the rumors. Daily they saw groups of Indians ride around the fort just out of rifle range, making their obscene and contemptuous gestures, yelling taunts that could be heard but not understood.

Most of the men longed for Custer's return, believing him capable, if anyone was, of leading a successful campaign against the Indians. Others, remembering Custer's behavior more than a year ago, behavior that had led to his court-martial, stoutly maintained that he would be no better than Sully, and might indeed be worse.

They cited the charges upon which he had been convicted: He had disregarded his orders and deserted his command. By his rebellious dash to join his wife, after the desertion of his command, he had damaged horses belonging to the U.S. government. He had neither pursued Indians who had attacked his escort, nor had he recovered the bodies of the soldiers killed. Earlier, he had ordered his officers to pursue and shoot down deserters and to bring none in alive. Obedient officers had actually shot these deserters. One of those shot had died of his wounds. The court also found him guilty of refusing to permit the wounded men to receive medical attention after their return to the command.

Could such a man, they argued, command the respect of his men? Could he lead them against the Indians who outnumbered them two or three to one and maybe more?

Holley tried to stay out of the arguments, many of which got hot enough to end in fisticuffs. One man was knifed, though superficially, and his assailant confined to the stockade for thirty days. Once Holley said to Frank, "If we'd had an army like this during the war, the Rebs would have whipped the hell out of us."

"They damn near did the first couple of years of the war."

Holley shrugged. He bitterly regretted joining the Army, considering the way things had turned out, considering too the prospects for the future. A dozen times every day he contemplated desertion, and sometimes discussed it with Frank. But each time he decided against it because he had no other workable alternative. At the very least, he hoped the Army would get him close to the Indian village where Julia was being held. Then would be time enough to desert, when there was a chance of rescuing her and getting her safely away.

So he waited, and fumed, and hoped. And Julia was never out of his thoughts.

When she had awakened to the sound of rifle fire, Julia had guessed, wildly, that Clay and Tom Denton had somehow raised a force to pursue and rescue them. Perhaps it was the U. S. Army out there surrounding the Indian camp.

Sally seized Frankie and started to get up and run, but Julia seized her legs with both arms and brought her to the ground. She knew that if the Indians saw them and thought they were getting away, they'd shoot them down.

Sally cried, "Let me go! Let me go! Tom's out there!"

"If he is, he'll come after us. In the meantime, if the Indians see us running away, we're going to get shot."

But the firing died away, and a group of Indians ran toward someone who had been hidden by darkness out there about a hundred yards away. She heard the rapid pound of horses' hoofs and then, from the other side of camp, heard the thunder of many hoofs. It sounded as if the whole Indian pony herd was being driven away.

She stayed close to the ground, holding Sally there. Sally kept trying to keep Frankie from crying, with only limited success.

The Indians returned on foot from their pursuit of their stolen pony herd. A couple of them seized torches from the fires and hurried away to examine the tracks of the horse thieves. When they came back, they were raging. One, drawing his knife, started toward Julia, Sally, and Frankie. Julia knew their time had come. Clay and Tom had tried to rescue them and had failed, but they had managed to drive off the entire Indian pony herd. Now this angry Indian was going to kill all three of them in revenge.

She had often wondered how she would feel, facing certain death. Now she knew. She was afraid, of course, but not nearly as afraid as she had thought she'd be. She discovered that the thought of death, when balanced against the prospect of living out the rest of her life with these Indians, was not unpleasant at all. She stood up and faced the approaching Indian, holding his angry glance with her own calm, steady one. The knife would hurt, but it would not hurt long.

On the ground behind her, Sally crouched, white-faced, silenced by the raw terror that she felt. Frankie whimpered but did not cry.

The Indian stopped while still a dozen feet from Julia. Julia had, until now, thought the Indians' faces inscrutable. Now she realized that had only been because she had not been around them much. The face of this Indian with the knife was in no way inscrutable. The anger, which had blazed earlier from his eyes, faded slowly and reluctantly. In its place came uncertainty, as if the courage he was seeing in this white squaw both confused and puzzled him. Lastly, as he stood there facing her, a kind of grudging admiration came into his face.

They faced each other for what seemed an eternity. Then, with a noncommittal grunt, the Indian sheathed the knife, turned on his heel, and stalked away.

Julia felt drained of strength. She had steeled herself to die. Discovering she was not going to die unnerved her. Her knees began to tremble violently. Tears sprang into her eyes.

Behind her, Sally began to weep hysterically, muffling the sound of her weeping as best she could by holding her hands up over her mouth. Once more Julia found strength within herself. She couldn't stop the trembling of her knees. But she could prevent herself from breaking down. She crouched and took Frankie into her arms to comfort him and, hopefully, to keep him from making any further noise. To Sally she whispered, "It's all right. It's all right now."

Sally continued to weep, but the Indians were too busy now to notice them. Leaving half a dozen behind to guard the captives, the others set out on foot at a steady trot after the stolen horses.

And Julia knew exactly who had been out there. Clay had come home to find them gone and the house burned. He had trailed the Indians a couple of hundred miles, to this place. He had tried to rescue them, but something had gone wrong.

She thought of Clay, and tears came into her eyes. He had risked everything to get to her. And she somehow knew that he would come again. It might be weeks or even months, but he would come again. And again. Until he was dead, or until she was.

She knew how worried he would be, how fearful that harm had come to her as a result of his abortive attempt to rescue her. She wished desperately that there was some way she could let him know she was all right.

But there was not. No way. Any more than there was any way for her to know whether one of the Indians bullets had found its mark in him.

All she could do was pray. She closed her eyes, lifted her face, and prayed more fervently than ever before in her life.

And when she had finished, she knew how much there was to be thankful for. She was alive. Her child was still inside her, safe and unhurt. Sally and Frankie, while utterly terrified, were still all right.

What Julia needed now was faith, abundant faith. That God would help Clay and Tom rescue them. That God would show them a way.

CHAPTER
ELEVEN

Before Custer's return to his regiment, and possibly either at his suggestion or upon his orders, the 7th was marched south to Bluff Creek, thirty miles from Dodge, where they pitched their tents and made camp. Clay Holley was elated at the move even though nothing was said about another campaign against the Indians.

But he guessed that this had to be part of the preparations. Custer was coming and Custer, despite his own cavalier attitude toward the orders of his superiors, was known as a strict disciplinarian. If anyone could, Custer would whip the 7th into a fighting force.

The fall days came and went. At last, in early October, Custer's long-awaited return became a reality. He arrived at a gallop, with two staghounds, named Maida and Blucher, loping along beside his horse, followed by his escort.

Custer's yellow hair whipped in the breeze. His fringed buckskins made him look like anything but a line officer in the United States Army.

The first thing he did was order an inspection, and he rode along the lines of shabby, weary, disillusioned, and poorly mounted men, scowling, impatient, with anger showing in his eyes.

What was said later at a staff meeting, Clay Holley and the other men could only guess. But on the day following, things began to change. Instead of lying around their tents all day, the men were ordered out for roll call immediately after breakfast. Their horses were inspected, as were they themselves, with stern reprimands for those who were sloppy or whose horses were not in shape.

There followed an entire day of drill, both mounted and on foot. When nightfall came, the men ate listlessly and wearily sought their beds.

The following day was the same, and the day following that. And all the while, as the columns of horsemen wheeled and turned, galloped and trotted and walked, the Indians watched from the distant hills.

As though to show their contempt for anything the pony soldiers could do, on the third evening the Indians launched an attack. Screeching, their paint and feathers brilliant in the setting sun, a solid line of red horsemen bore down upon the camp.

The pickets knelt and, as the line of Indians came close, opened fire, emptying their guns at the advancing horde. A few horses fell. Their riders were scooped up by other Indians and the screaming line came on.

Custer came out of his tent and strode back and forth, bellowing at his officers and at the men. For several minutes, the camp was bedlam.

Holley snatched up a carbine and ran toward the side of the camp where the Indians were making their attack. He arrived in time to see the long line divide in the middle. Half the Indians swept around the camp on one side, half on the other. When they reached the opposite side of camp, the pickets on that side also began firing.

Two kicking horses lay fifty yards from the edge of camp. Apparently not an Indian had been hit. Nor had the Indians had any better luck. A couple of troopers had superficial flesh wounds, but that was all.

Well past the camp, out of effective rifle range, the entire force of Indians hauled their sweating ponies to a halt. From their backs they screeched taunts at the soldiers.

It was obvious they wanted to be pursued, and Holley guessed that an even larger force of Indians waited somewhere beyond the nearest hills. It was also obvious to him that Custer wanted to pursue, that he restrained himself only because of the condition of his troops and their low morale.

But that night, under cover of first darkness, Custer ordered four columns to probe the surrounding countryside, scouting along the streams, in an attempt to locate and destroy the village from which the Indians had come.

Holley and Frank Denton rode with part of G Troop, scouting west along Bluff Creek. They rode at a steady trot until midnight, without finding anything.

California Joe led the column with which Holley and Frank Denton rode. He had just that day been appointed by Custer as chief of scouts, and had imbibed freely in celebration before leaving camp. He had, furthermore, brought along a canteen filled with whiskey instead of water, and as the night progressed, he drank frequently from the canteen.

Just before turning back, Major Elliott, commanding the column, sent California Joe on ahead to scout a sharp bend in the creek. The scout left, canteen in hand, swaying in the saddle. Holley said sourly to Frank, "He'd better hope he don't find any Indians, the shape he's in."

At the bend, the column halted to wait for California Joe's return. It wasn't long in coming. California Joe came riding at a jogging trot through the brush and trees that lined the stream bed, singing to himself in a low voice that nevertheless carried more than fifty yards.

Suddenly Joe saw the halted column of troopers ahead of him. In his drunken surprise, he mistook the column for Indians. He halted his horse, hesitated only an instant, and then, with a wild war whoop, spurred his horse directly toward the column, dropping his canteen, pumping round after round from his Spencer at the dark shapes waiting in the trees.

Major Elliott bawled angrily, "You damn fool, it's us!" and the cry was taken up by at least a dozen men. Joe hauled his horse to a sudden halt.

Clay Holley muttered disgustedly. "Some scout! And Custer just made him chief of scouts!"

Joe came on, crestfallen and embarrassed. Elliott told him shortly, "I intend to report this conduct to the general. I doubt if you'll have your post as chief of scouts for very long. I doubt if you can even hold onto your job as scout." He turned his head and called back to the men, "Is anybody hit?"

Nobody replied. Elliott told the scout, "You're lucky. If you'd hurt anyone there'd have been hell to pay. All right, lead us back to camp. If you think you can find it in the dark."

A sullen and silent California Joe took the lead and the long line of weary troopers followed in a column a quarter of a mile long.

It was long after midnight when they reached the camp. The troopers fell out, cared for their mounts, and then fell exhaustedly into their beds. California Joe, much more sober now, disappeared in the direction of the tents where the scouts slept.

Holley lay there thinking for a long time. He'd never seen such a sorry collection of would-be soldiers in his life. In their present state, they couldn't whip an equal number of Indian women, let alone Indian men.

The next day, the drills continued, even more rigorous than before. From dawn to dark, the men drilled. The lathered horses were halted from time to time, cooled and rubbed down by the men. Custer seemed to be trying to simulate conditions as they would be when he actually marched against the Indians.

Although no ammunition had been designated by the Army for target practice, Custer used it nevertheless. In prone, sitting, and standing positions, the men fired endlessly at targets, until most of them could hit a target the size of a man at a hundred and fifty yards four times out of five, a target as large as a horse at three hundred yards.

Sully protested the use of the ammunition, saying it would be needed later when they engaged the Indians. Custer replied shortly and contemptuously that it wouldn't make a damned bit of difference how much ammunition the troopers had when they engaged the Indians if they couldn't hit anything.

Holley began to feel a little hope. Custer *was* apparently going after the Indians as soon as the Indian summer weather broke and winter finally set in. The first good snowstorm would, he was sure, see the 7th on the march.

Then Holley would think of Sand Creek, the so-called "battle" that had happened four years ago. A regiment of Colorado Volunteers had marched against a Cheyenne and Arapaho village just west of the Kansas line and had attacked the village in the predawn hours while all the Indians were asleep.

It had been slaughter, with Indians — men, women, and children — dying before they even had time to dress. The few survivors had straggled away from the scene leaving a trail of blood and the bodies of those who died along the way.

That massacre was largely responsible for all the trouble the Indians were causing now. Holley knew, furthermore, that if the Indians at Sand Creek had been holding any white prisoners, they would not have survived the first ten minutes of the attack.

It was this that worried him. Custer had just returned to his regiment from a year's suspension resulting from his court-martial conviction. He was on trial with his superiors with the possible exception of Phil Sheridan, in whose eyes he apparently could do no wrong. Desperately he wanted to restore the luster to his tarnished reputation. And he would do whatever he thought was necessary to accomplish it.

Which meant he would somehow manage to find an Indian village, attack, and wipe it out the way the Colorado Volunteers had destroyed the one at Sand Creek. There would be no opportunity for Holley and Frank Denton to get in ahead of the troops, no opportunity for them to find the two women and Tom Denton's son, no chance to rescue them if they happened to be there.

Night after night Holley lay awake, searching his thoughts for an alternative. There wasn't one. His only chance of rescuing the women and Frankie lay in going along with the troops. But perhaps when the battle began, a chance would present itself. Not a praying or churchgoing man, Holley prayed now. He prayed for the life of his wife and unborn child. He prayed for Tom Denton's wife and son. And he prayed that when the time came, he would be shown a way to rescue them before they all were killed.

As a means of instilling pride into the troops, Custer issued mounts of a uniform color to each troop. G Troop received bay horses. Other troops received brown, dun, or gray. The band, in deference to Sheridan, whose band had always been so mounted, received gray horses.

103

Furthermore, the men were carefully screened during target practice, and near the end of October a special sharpshooter corps was formed and placed under the command of Lieutenant Cook. Clay Holley was among the first chosen for this corps, as was Frank Denton.

And now, daily, wagon trains arrived from Fort Dodge, carrying supplies. The men were issued winter uniforms, heavy boots, fur caps, and greatcoats even though the weather still was warm.

Custer was always highly visible, riding to and fro on his high-spirited prancing charger, or striding back and forth impatiently on foot, shrilly shouting criticism, counsel, or praise for those who excelled.

Holley had not believed it possible, but out of the confusion, out of the murderously long days of hard work, out of Custer's criticism came a strange cohesiveness — pride — esprit de corps. The men began to feel proud of the way they could perform. Target practice became competitive. And now when the Indians shouted their taunts from the nearby hills, the troopers shouted tautingly back at them.

At last, the first week of November, a cold wind began blowing out of the north. Dark gray clouds scudded swiftly along, close to the ground. A few snowflakes fell, and some sleet, but hardly enough to cover the ground.

As though by magic, the Indians who had taunted them so long, disappeared. Nobody needed to be told where they had gone. They had headed south into Indian Territory, as they always did when winter threatened. They would seek out their villages and remain there, except for an occasional hunting foray, until spring melted the snow and greened the grass again.

To Holley, the onslaught of winter meant that this column, which had been preparing so long and so diligently, would move. Perhaps not immediately. But within a couple of weeks, depending on the weather, they would finally begin their march south toward the Indian villages.

He discovered that he had mixed feelings about going. On the one hand, he was desperately anxious to go, to be given a chance to rescue his wife and Tom Denton's wife and boy. On the other hand, he was desperately afraid that their going, that their attack when they finally found a village big enough to justify one, would be the direct cause of his wife's and Sally Denton's death.

Honed to a sharp edge of readiness, Clay and the others of the 7th watched the skies and listened to the wind, and waited for the day when they would march.

CHAPTER
TWELVE

That first November storm, inconsequential though it was, galvanized Custer and, through him, all the officers under him. A great, canvas-topped wagon train began to assemble, along with mules to pull the wagons. Four hundred of them there were, with four mules to each wagon and a couple of hundred spares.

The wagons were loaded with everything imaginable that might be needed on what everyone expected to be a long campaign. Ammunition. Rations, blankets, clothing. Hay and grain for horses that might not be able to forage if the snow was deep.

The men themselves were ready now, even according to Custer's exacting requirements. They could shoot; they had been given enough target practice to make sure of that. They could march, and control their mounts under all forseeable conditions; they had been drilled long enough to make sure of that. Whether they could fight or not would be determined when they finally reached their objective in Indian Territory to the south.

Finally, at dawn on November 12 the ponderous column moved out. California Joe, who had been demoted from his position as chief of scouts after the drunken episode a month earlier, rode at the head of the column with Custer, along with other white scouts and some Osage trackers. Behind Custer rode the corps of sharpshooters under Lieutenant Cook, of which both Clay Holley and Frank Denton were a part. The band on their gray horses came next, and behind the band the other troops. The wagon train, ponderous and unbelievably long, followed, commanded by General Sully, who rode, as he customarily did, in an ambulance.

The skies were overcast and a chill wind blew out of the north. Overhead, black clouds scudded along on the increasing wind. Holley and Denton rode abreast in the column of twos.

Neither had much to say, each being immersed in his own private thoughts. Both knew, as indeed did all the men, that they were riding into Indian Territory, into land reserved for the Indians and controlled by the reservation agents there. Both knew, as did all the men, that General Hazen had been sent earlier to the agents with money for the Indians' keep during the winter months.

Nobody among the troops knew, if indeed did any among the officers, how they were going to tell peaceful Indians from hostile ones.

To Holley, after what had been done to him and to his wife by a small band of hostiles, it didn't really make any difference. He and his family had been peaceful, a threat to no one. He didn't really give a damn whether there were innocents in whatever village or villages they attacked. He was prepared to kill whatever Indians stood between him and the rescue of his wife.

The long column halted at noon, less than half a dozen miles from their starting point. Custer rode back and forth impatiently as the men built small fires, made coffee, cooked bacon, and fried hardtack in the grease. Once he rode to the head of the supply column, where he conferred briefly with Sully.

The band played "Garry Owen" as soon as they had reassembled, and shortly afterward the whole regiment rode out again. The snow thickened as they rode until by midafternoon there was an inch or so on the ground.

And now Custer sent his scouts ranging out on both sides of the column and ahead searching for a trail. They disappeared into the driving snow.

At dusk, the regiment halted for the night. They bivouacked in the bed of a dry stream where there was firewood, water if a man dug in the sandy stream bed for it, and some shelter from the wind.

Holley and Frank Denton shared the same fire, along with two other members of the sharpshooter corps. The four crouched around it, boiling coffee, frying bacon. One of the other men, Ed Hines, said, "At this rate, we ain't likely to find us any Indians before Christmas comes."

Holly said, "Ten miles a day. It isn't much, but ten days is a hundred miles. We'll find us some Indians sure enough."

Hines said, "I heard they took your wife. Think we got any chance of finding her?"

Clay said, "I hope. But there's bound to be a lot of Indian villages in the reservation and she could be in any one of them. The chances of us finding the right one aren't too good, I guess."

"What will you do if we don't find her in whatever village we attack?"

Clay looked across the fire at Frank. He said, "I guess we'll stay with the regiment as long as they stay in Indian Territory."

Hines didn't need to be told what Clay and Frank intended to do if the regiment did not. He said, "I'll tell you something, boys. I was with that sonofabitch Custer when he had those deserters shot a year ago before they court-martialed him. I don't figure to serve any more time under him than I have to. So if you boys decide to desert and go after your women, and you got sense enough to do it so's we don't get caught, then I reckon I wouldn't mind coming along with you."

Clay stared across the fire, a burning sensation in his throat. There were things he might have said, but he only nodded. "Appreciate it. And I accept your offer." He waited a moment and finally he said, "That don't do justice to what I feel. I hope you know that."

Hines nodded. "I know."

The other man, Lester Daniels, spoke up. "Reckon you can count me in too. One of them deserters Custer ordered shot was a friend of mine. Besides, I been figuring on going down Texas way to get me a job on a ranch. Maybe it won't pay no more than the Army does, but a man don't have to take so damn much crap from a bunch of bastards wearing a little gold who think they're God." Both Daniels and Hines made excuses for what they were offering to do but it wasn't entirely hatred for Custer that made them willing to desert.

Clay didn't tell Daniels that he had been one of those bastards wearing a little gold during the war. He just nodded his acceptance of the offer. He said, "Four men sure as hell will be better than two." He looked across the fire at Daniels, the gratitude he was feeling in his eyes.

They fried hardtack in the bacon grease, finished their meal, and let the fire die to a bed of coals. The four, now welded by a common purpose, wrapped their blankets around them and lay down to sleep. Clay Holley stayed awake for a while, thinking of Hines and Daniels and of the unhesitating way both had offered to desert in order to help him find and rescue his wife. Then, feeling more hopeful than he had in a long time, he finally went to sleep.

Two more days of travel followed, through occasionally spitting snow or sleet, over ground covered by an inch to two inches of snow. Not enough to impede the march but enough to clearly see any tracks that had been made in the last three days.

At last, on the sixth day out, where the column crossed Beaver Creek, the scouts brought Custer news of an Indian trail.

Since Sully had been placed in command of the column on its march to establish a new Army post, Camp Supply, in Indian Territory, Custer was obliged to ride back to the supply train, locate Sully's ambulance, and ask him for permission to pursue.

Neither Holley, Denton, Hines, nor Daniels had any way of knowing what transpired or what was said; they could only guess by observing the flushed and furious face of Custer as he galloped his horse forward along the halted column of twos to the head of them once more. Clay said, "Sully said no."

"Sure as hell. And Custer don't like it one damn bit," Ed Hines said.

Denton asked, "You reckon we'll be under Sully's command all the way? If we are, we'd just as well forget about fighting Indians. He'll find a way to avoid running into any."

"Sheridan's supposed to meet us at the new camp."

"And Custer's Sheridan's favorite. Chances are old Phil will put Custer in command."

"I sure as hell hope he does." And the column lumbered on toward its destination.

When the first cold wind came whistling down out of the north and when the first stinging particles of sleet began to cover the ground, the village where Julia Holley and Sally Denton were being held captive prepared to move.

Horses were brought in, and the travois poles secured to their backs. Everything inside each tipi was stored in parfleches, of which each family had many, for transport on the travois. Most of the parfleches were old, darkened with smoke and from handling, but on each was a bright painted geometric design. Blankets and robes were folded and those that were not expected to be used were tied in bundles. Food supplies, mostly consisting of dried meat and berries, were similarly packed. Lastly the tipis came down, were folded, and were placed on the travois. Nothing was left behind that was usable. When the column finally moved out away from the village site, only a few broken children's toys were left behind, and at the edge of camp a pile of bones, partially scattered by the dogs.

Julia, even though she was now very heavy with her child, nevertheless was able to do her share, a necessity if she wanted to avoid being beaten by the other squaws.

She had been taken, a month after her capture, as the wife of one of the warriors who had captured her. He was a man of about thirty-five, tall, as were many of the Cheyennes, muscular, and well thought of in the village. His name was Short Dog.

She slept in his lodge, along with his other squaw and his two children, one a baby, the other about two years old. He made no attempt to have intercourse with her. Perhaps, she thought, intercourse with a pregnant woman was taboo. Giving support to this theory was the fact that none of the Indians who had originally captured her had made any attempt to molest her, though they had raped Sally Denton repeatedly, until Sally was hysterical and eventually numb, as though her mind had blocked out what was happening to her.

She had remained numb and unspeaking for a long time afterward. Frankie was, perhaps, the one who had

112

brought her out of it, with his fright and crying and his obvious need of the comfort only she could give.

Sally had also been taken as the wife of one of the braves that had captured them. Julia didn't know what his demands on Sally were, having no way of knowing what went on in the lodge where Sally lived. And Sally never talked of it. In fact Sally rarely talked of anything and Julia could tell that she had given up all hope of ever being rescued from the Indians.

Julia told herself firmly, over and over again, that she would never give up hope. Clay and Tom Denton had been forced to flee the night they had tried rescuing their wives to avoid certain death. But she had faith in Clay and she knew he would be back. She knew that she and their unborn child were the most important things in the world to Clay. She knew he would never rest until he had either rescued her or verified her death.

In the meantime, she made up her mind that she would make the best of what had happened to her. The work was harder than it had been on the ranch, but she was strong and nothing was demanded of her that she couldn't do. She was afraid of the time when she would be forced to bear her baby here among these Indians, but she had seen how easily they accomplished it. All the women who were needed pitched in to help, and mothers and babies both seemed to come through the ordeal fine.

Southward, roughly following the bed of the stream upon which they had been camped, the little column traveled. On the second day, they joined another similar column coming from the west. Julia guessed they were heading for a winter camp. She also guessed that the winter camp would be a large one, perhaps containing hundreds, even thousands of Indians.

There were days when the sun would break through the clouds for a little while. The ground was warm, and its warmth rapidly melted the snow that fell. But each day the wind grew colder; each day the clouds became heavier. And finally a day came, by Julia's reckoning close to the second week in November, when the snow began to fall in earnest.

On that day they reached their destination, an enormous series of villages clustered on the bank of a stream she was told was the Washita. Their own small group found a spot where they could camp and they halted, unpacked the travois, and began erecting the tipis.

Six inches of snow lay on the ground and it had to be cleared before the tipis could be set up. There were visitors constantly coming and going from the camp, helping with the work, visiting old friends.

In a remarkably short time, the job was done. Fires were built inside the newly erected tipis and meals prepared. Life went on as usual.

But a new fear was now growing in Julia. So large was this collection of villages that Clay and Tom would have no chance of rescuing them, even assuming it would be possible for their husbands to locate them.

CHAPTER
THIRTEEN

It was a sullen and angry George Armstrong Custer who led his troops on south toward Camp Supply. Supply was roughly one hundred miles from Dodge across country. With the ponderous column of four hundred supply wagons to slow them down, they were lucky to make ten miles a day.

Finally, however, after a week of traveling, they reached Wolf Creek just above its confluence with the Beaver. Here they halted, and set up new Camp Supply.

Custer, being unwilling to go on as a subordinate of Sully's, who, he claimed, was inferior to him in rank, began to rebel openly. The two men wrangled loudly and angrily far into the night. Both, it appeared, had been commissioned permanent lieutenant colonels on the same day, which placed them on an equal footing so far as their present rank was concerned.

Custer argued, however, this his brevet wartime rank of major general outranked Sully's brevet wartime rank of brigadier. But Sully stubbornly refused to surrender command of the regiment.

It became a stalemate, with both men refusing to budge. Custer couldn't lead the regiment south against specific orders, and Sully was apparently unwilling to assume the responsibility of leading the regiment alone, because he doubted his own capabilities.

However, since Sheridan was expected at Camp Supply within two or three days, the stalemate was allowed to continue. The men took advantage of the time to rest and recuperate. The horses and mules were allowed to graze under guard, and at night were each fed a generous amount of oats.

Rumors flew thick and fast among the waiting men. Some said Sully would win out and that they would flounder around for a week or two and finally return to Dodge without engaging any hostiles.

Others claimed that Custer would win out, that he was Phil Sheridan's pet and would be given the command. If that happened, they said, they would find Indians if they had to comb every square inch south of the Kansas line. Furthermore, if they did find Indians, and if Custer was in command at the time, the victory would be decisive and complete. Custer was eager to restore the luster to his tarnished reputation, and only a major victory could accomplish that.

Finally, three days after their arrival at Camp Supply, a column of cavalry was sighted approaching from the east. Custer immediately called for his horse, and fretted impatiently while he waited for it to be saddled and brought to him. The column drew closer. Sully came from his tent and watched, apparently willing to wait until Sheridan arrived to present his case.

The men, Clay Holley, Denton, Hines, and Daniels included, watched with interest. Custer's horse was finally brought to him. He mounted and, flanked by the two frolicking and excited staghounds Maida and Blucher, rode out to intercept the approaching column.

Sheridan, recognizable even at this distance by his short stature and by the lumpy way he sat his saddle, halted the column and shook hands enthusiastically with Custer. The two men talked for a while, then dismounted and squatted on the ground to talk some more. Custer appeared to be drawing on the ground with a stick.

Holley said, "He's laying out his battle plan. It's going to be Custer, that's sure as hell. Sully made a fool of himself and of the whole regiment last time he went out."

Hines said, "I'll have to agree with that. Besides, Sheridan likes Custer for some damn reason or other. He's about the only general officer who does, though."

"It's a funny thing," said Daniels. "Custer made just as big a fool of himself on his last campaign as Sully did. He was out after Indians and they outfought him and mocked him every inch of the way. He lost men and once he admitted himself that forty men deserted between taps and reveille. But I guess what really got him in bad was that he took about seventy-five men as an escort and left his command floundering around while he hotfooted it back to Fort Riley to see his wife."

"Had some deserters shot too, didn't he?"

Daniels nodded. "Major Elliott and Lieutenant Cook were the ones who did the shooting too." He grinned. "That ought to be a warning for all four of us."

Out on the plain, half a mile from Camp Supply, Custer and Sheridan squatted on the ground, surrounded by Sheridan's staff. Custer was drawing on the ground. With a stick, he drew their present position, then, to the south, drew the winding course of Wolf Creek, and farther south the Canadian River, and still farther south the Washita. Far southeast along the course of the Washita, he made an X to represent the Indian Agency. North of this X he drew a whole series of small Xs and glancing up he said, "They're there. I'm sure of it. Or they will be as soon as the snow covers up the grass."

"What's the trouble between you and Sully?" asked Sheridan.

"Hell, the man doesn't want to fight. He rides in that damned ambulance of his and he doesn't even know what's going on. We struck an Indian trail on the way down here and I asked for permission to follow it and was refused. General, if you send this command south under Sully, they'll flounder around the same way they did before I arrived and they'll come back here out of rations, with half their wagons and horses gone and nothing to show for it."

Sheridan got to his feet. "Did you know that Sully was one of those who urged your reinstatement?"

Custer looked briefly ashamed. Then, almost sullenly he said, "General, the fact remains that he can't whip the Indians. He's had his chance. You should have seen this regiment when I rejoined it several weeks ago."

Both men were standing now, Sheridan short and blocky, Custer taller, slimmer.

Sheridan nodded finally. "All right. I'll put you in command. I'll send Sully back to Fort Dodge."

Custer's face was flushed with triumph. "When can we leave?"

"As soon as the rest of the 19th Kansas arrives. They're on their way from Topeka now."

Custer's face mirrored short-lived disappointment. He had won his victory over Sully and was now in sole command of the 7th Cavalry. He would take up the matter of the 19th Kansas later, if they did not arrive within a day or two. He mounted, as did Sheridan, and the column continued its march toward Camp Supply.

Sully came from his tent and walked to meet Sheridan. The two shook hands and talked briefly. It was immediately apparent to the men that Sully had been relieved of his command. His face was red, his strides quick and angry ones.

Clay Holley watched Custer turn to walk away. Sully spoke to him. Custer hesitated. Sheridan, after a swift glance from one of the men to the other, turned and walked away himself toward the spot where some of the men of the 19th Kansas Volunteers were already erecting his tent.

Sully was obviously furious. Equally obvious was the fact that Custer would like to get away. But there was no graceful way he could accomplish it, so he followed Sully into his tent.

An angry harangue by Sully followed, the words indistinguishable because of the muffling effect the canvas had. Occasionally Custer's voice would be heard, softer, with a placating tone. But Sully must have said something intemperate because at last, Custer stormed from the tent, as furious as Holley had ever seen him, even when he had been refused permission to follow the Indian trail.

Sully did not delay his departure for Fort Dodge very long. Before midafternoon his tent had been struck, the men who were to escort him assembled and mounted. Riding hidden in his ambulance, Sully took the long trail north toward Dodge, a score of troopers out ahead, a score bringing up the rear. Three supply wagons jolted along behind the ambulance.

Holley watched the column until it disappeared from sight over a long rise of ground. He turned to Denton and said, "Now all we've got to do is wait."

"For how long?"

Holley glanced at the gray and threatening sky. The wind was bitter, if not very strong. "Two or three days. If the rest of the 19th Kansas isn't here by then, I figure Custer will go on without them. Particularly if it snows."

That night, the band of the 7th Cavalry formed outside Phil Sheridan's tent to serenade him. They played all of Custer's perennial favorites, "Garry Owen," "The Girl I Left Behind Me," "Ain't I Glad to Get Out of the Wilderness," "Oralee," and others.

Clay Holley lay unsleeping in his tent. The strains of "Oralee" brought a tightness to his throat because it was a melody his mind always connected with Julia.

And as he listened, a deep depression came over him. Fear that he would never see her again turned his body cold. There were thousands of Indians scattered over thousands of square miles in Indian Territory south of here.

There were Indian camps on every stream, thousands of buffalo-hide lodges. Only God could lead them to the right village or cluster of villages. Only God could lead him to the village where Julia was, to the lodge where she might be.

Clay had never thought very much about God, although Julia had been very religious and had read the Bible every night. He found it hard even now to place all his faith in God. Used to depending on himself, he wished that now he could still depend only on himself.

But it wasn't possible. He was in the Army, subject to army discipline, and he would go wherever Custer took the 7th Cavalry. When the Indians were engaged, he would follow the orders of Lieutenant Cook. He would not be free to go off on his own searching for his wife.

Reason and good sense told him what he had undertaken was impossible. Then he thought of Julia. He remembered her face, the calmness in her eyes, her body, heavy and awkward with their child. Her faith in him would never waver, and neither could he let his faith in himself waver.

But faith in himself was not enough. This once, regardless of all that he had believed or not believed in the past, he would have to trust in God. To lead him across the miles to the village where Julia was. To provide an opportunity for him to rescue her once they had arrived.

Already, he thought, some power over which he had no control had provided him with help. Hines had agreed to go with him, even if it meant deserting and risking the penalties for that. So had Daniels.

And why had those two volunteered to help? There was no logical answer he could find within himself. They owed him nothing. He hadn't even known them long.

His wavering faith began to strengthen. Perhaps God, who, they said, worked his wonders in mysterious ways, was already doing so.

The band stopped playing and the bugler sounded the clear, sweet tones of taps.

The camp grew quiet. There was the usual night sounds, the calls of the sentries indicating that all was well, the barking of a dog occasionally, probably one of Custer's staghounds or maybe one of the mongrels that lived around the camp, the occasional shrill whinny of a horse as a kicking and biting scuffle took place.

Clay finally went to sleep. And dreamed of Julia, once more in his arms.

CHAPTER
FOURTEEN

A day passed, cold and blustery with the wind laden with stinging flakes of snow. As was the case every day the troops were mustered, the roll called, the horses inspected, and a mounted drill ordered which lasted until noon.

Custer watched from his tent. Finally he walked over to Sheridan's tent and disappeared inside.

Sheridan was edgy because of the delay in the arrival of the rest of the 19th Kansas from Topeka. "I don't know where the hell the sonsabitches are. They've had plenty of time to get here."

Custer voiced the obvious. "Maybe they're lost, General."

"If they are, by God . . ." Sheridan didn't finish.

Custer said, "We don't need them, General. The 7th can whip all the Indians we're likely to find south of here."

"Like Sully whipped them a month ago?" Sheridan's tone was sarcastic.

Custer reminded him: "I'm not Sully, General. And besides, the hostiles are going to be camped by the time we get to them. Let me take the 7th and go, General. I won't let you down."

"Damn you, you'd better not. Grant would like nothing better than to have your scalp. Sherman urged your reinstatement, but make one mistake and he'll be after your hide along with everybody else."

"Except you, General. I want you to know I appreciate your faith."

Sheridan, dour and unsmiling, nevertheless managed to convey approval with his glance. He said, "Have you got a plan?"

"Yes, sir. I want to march south, up Wolf Creek and across to the Canadian, and then on to the Washita."

"That's where the Indian Agency is. You don't plan to attack them there?"

"No sir. I don't figure they're at the Indian Agency. They're probably thirty or forty miles on this side of it."

Sheridan's eyes took on a gleam. Custer knew well what Sheridan thought of Indians. He'd said often enough that the only good Indian was a dead one, and while he might not have said so publicly, he made, in his mind, no distinction as to age or sex.

"All right, what have you got in mind?"

"We'll march south. Hopefully the way the weather looks, it will snow. If we're lucky, by the time we get there there'll be at least a foot of snow."

Sheridan said, "I don't want you to sting them and then let them get away."

"No, sir. I don't plan on anything like that. What I figure on is a surround. So none of them can get away."

Sheridan considered that. If what Custer had just suggested was possible, and if he did catch the Indians by surprise, asleep in camp, maybe he could wipe them out and end this goddamned Indian problem once and for all. He made up his mind suddenly. "All right! We won't wait for the 19th. You take your 7th Cavalry and go ahead."

"What are my orders, General?" Custer couldn't conceal either his elation or his excitement.

Sherman was very blunt. "Proceed south in the direction of the Antelope Hills, thence on toward the Washita. Find and destroy their villages. Kill their ponies. Kill or hang all warriors and bring back all women and children as prisoners."

Those were the orders, but both Custer and Sheridan knew they were impossible. Even if caught by surprise, the Indians would fight. Women often fought as ferociously as the men. Children would be caught in the crossfire.

The motives of the two men might be different, but their purpose was the same. Sheridan wanted to be rid of the Indian problem once and for all. He was tired of catching hell from his superiors, tired of the criticism of congressmen and other politicians every time a white family got wiped out. He had got to the point where he didn't give a damn how it was done just so it was done. He liked Custer. He knew it was said that Custer was his pet. But he also knew the recklessness that Custer possessed. He knew that if Custer found the Indians he would attack and to hell with the odds, whatever they might be.

Custer, on the other hand, had been deeply hurt by the court-martial verdict more than a year ago. At the time it had seemed to be the end of his military career.

He had moped and fretted throughout the year of suspension, moody, surly at times, unpredictable, but always showing a cheerful façade to the press and to anyone who visited him and Libby in Monroe.

Reinstatement had driven him nearly hysterical with joy. He had leaped and shouted, and tossed Libby into the air and hugged her until she could hardly breathe. And now at last he had his chance. Leading his beloved 7th, he was to march south against the Indian villages on the Washita. Almost in his grasp was the glorious victory he so desperately needed to restore the tarnished luster to his name and fame. Once more he would be the darling of the American people, the boy general the public so adored.

Custer's final word as he left Sheridan's tent was, "Tomorrow, General?"

Sheridan nodded. "Tomorrow. And dammit, don't you let me down!"

Custer emerged from Sheridan's tent in a state of ecstatic euphoria. It showed in the glow in his eyes, in the expression on his face. He issued crisp orders to the members of his staff waiting outside the tent.

Sheridan came to the flap. "Custer."

Custer turned. "Yes, General?"

"Here." Sheridan tendered the gifts awkwardly. They were a pair of buffalo shoes, a buffalo vest, and a fur cap. Sheridan said, "From my staff and me. With luck."

Custer accepted the gifts soberly. "Thank you, General, and thank your staff for me. I promise you again, sir, I will not let you down."

Sheridan grumped something that Custer couldn't hear. Then he disappeared into his tent again.

Custer crossed the parade, listening to the shouted orders he had given members of his staff being relayed down the line.

Having set the campaign in motion, having set the departure time, he went to his tent and sat down at his desk to write his wife.

The wind howled, gaining intensity as the afternoon wore on. Snow thickened but that only made Custer more jubilant. His best chance lay, he knew, in having the Indians immobilized by snow, eighteen inches if possible. He wanted to catch them all together. He wanted to wipe them out like a hill of ants.

His men were well armed with Spencer carbines, which held seven shells in the magazine and one in the chamber for a total of eight. This was the gun the Confederates had said the Yankees could load on Sunday and shoot all week. They were dressed and equipped for a severe winter campaign. Their horses were in good condition and the supply train of four hundred wagons carried enough ammunition, rations, extra clothing, blankets, and hay and grain for the horses to support a campaign lasting six weeks or more.

But Custer wasn't planning on six weeks. He intended to be back in Camp Supply, victorious, in half that length of time.

It was with extreme elation that Holley received the news that they would be leaving Camp Supply at dawn. The orders Sheridan had given Custer were known almost immediately by all the men. Holley knew one thing. They'd find their Indians.

His elation was, however, tempered with dread, as he thought, once again, of the Sand Creek massacre. He was afraid the situation would be no different when Custer found his prey. The attack would come at dawn. It would come from all sides at once. He and Denton and Hines and Daniels wouldn't have a prayer of getting into the village ahead of time.

Not unless, he thought, they went in the night before, ahead of the attack. But how in the hell could they manage that? Their coming, if discovered, would alert the Indians and result in the deaths of countless of their comrades when the troops attacked an awake and ready village instead of a sleeping one.

And even if they did get in, how in God's name could they find the lodges in which Julia and Sally Denton were being held? The answer was, they couldn't.

Luck and the will of God were going to decide whether he found Julia and Sally or not. Luck and the will of God would decide whether they rescued them or not.

And despite his desperate concern, he could not help thinking of all the innocents that were going to die. Women. Children. Even babes in arms.

There ought to be, he thought, better ways of settling things. The Indians made war on women and children. In retaliation, the Army did the same.

And in the end, no more would be settled than had been settled by Chivington at Sand Creek. Hatreds would only be bitterly intensified. Atrocities would increase.

Custer would be deliberately and knowingly violating the Medicine Lodge Treaty of 1867, which gave the Cheyennes, Arapahos, Comanches, and Kiowas the right to roam at will south of the Kansas line in peace.

But the redmen had already violated the spirit of the treaty by kidnapping white women and children and then carrying them south to the supposed safety of Indian Territory south of the Kansas line.

Holly wondered why the hell they bothered to make treaties at all. Nobody kept or respected them.

That night he and Denton, Hines, and Daniels met in the snow out in the middle of the parade. Already it lay four inches deep on the ground.

Denton asked, "What the hell are we going to do? We're not going to get a chance to get those women out."

Holley remembered Julia, remembered her strength and her intelligence. He said, "Maybe we'll get some help. Neither my wife nor Mrs. Denton is a fool. Maybe they'll play dead or hide out or something until they get a chance to let it be known that they're white."

Denton said, "By now, they probably look like squaws."

"Maybe so, but they haven't forgotten English. They can still cry out."

"And get shot by the Indians."

Holley looked at Denton disgustedly. "If you're so damn sure we're going to fail why bother to go along?"

"I just don't see . . ."

129

"Well, I don't see either, but I'm not giving up. I'm going to get my wife back no matter what I have to do."

He looked at Daniels and Hines. "What about you two?"

"We'll stick with you."

Holley asked, "Why? You'll probably get yourselves killed."

Hines said, "Nobody lives forever. Besides, I don't like the goddam Army very much. And I like that sonofabitch Custer even less."

Holley gripped Hines's shoulder and slapped Daniels on the back as they headed back through the snowstorm toward their tents.

CHAPTER
FIFTEEN

At four o'clock on November 23 the bugler blew reveille and the sleepy, grumbling men of the 7th Cavalry rolled out of their blankets, shook and folded them, struck their tents in darkness, and carried them to the wagons in which they would be transported south.

The sky was black as pitch. Not a star was visible. Great, wet flakes of snow filled the air, covering everything, soaking everything. On the ground was a foot of wet and sticky snow that made everything that had to be done seem doubly hard.

Sheridan came to the flap of his tent in his nightshirt, his hairy legs looking spindly beneath it, and bawled, "Custer! Goddammit, Custer, come here! I want to talk to you!"

Custer, who had sat up writing Libby until two, but who had been up for at least an hour, rode his prancing charger to the general's tent. Sheridan asked unbelievingly, "Jesus Christ, man, you've not going to leave in this muck, are you?"

Custer sounded surprised. "Why not, General? There isn't but a foot or so of snow on the ground."

131

"It's sure as hell going to get worse. Holy God, you can't see fifty feet."

"We'll be all right, General."

Sheridan shrugged hopelessly. "All right. But I think you're a goddam fool."

Custer grinned cheerfully, "Yes, sir, General."

Sheridan watched him ride away into the thickening, driving snow. He disappeared from his tent flap only to reappear several minutes later, dressed, wearing his boots and Union Cavalry campaign hat. He stood half in and half out of his tent, watching the preparations being made. Watching the half-awake troopers file in and out of the mess tent for their coffee and breakfast.

Nearly everything had been ready for days. The supply wagons were loaded, their canvas tops lashed down and secured against the snow. But the mules that were to pull them had to be harnessed and hitched to each wagon, a monumental job when you considered there were four hundred wagons, which added up to sixteen hundred mules. The racket was phenomenal, with at least two hundred of the mules braying at once, with men cursing and shouting, with equipment clanking, and with eleven troops of cavalry — seven hundred men, slogging through the snow, locating their mounts, saddling, mounting, trying to form into some kind of rank and order on the huge snow-enveloped parade.

Clay Holley and Frank Denton were among the first to be ready. Around them Lieutenant Cook's sharpshooters formed, trying to control their horses, to whom the excitement of the preparations had been conveyed.

Hines and Daniels showed up, along with the others of the forty designated as the sharpshooters' corps. Lieutenant Cook arrived and bawled, "Sergeant, call the roll!"

The sergeant's voice roared each name in turn, reading from a list he tried to protect from the falling snow by half concealing it beneath his greatcoat flap. Each man shouted his answer, and at last the roll call was complete.

Still, from the direction of the supply train, came the bitter, angry curses of the teamsters and the almost defiant braying of the mules.

Clay Holley, sitting his fidgeting horse in the thickly falling, soggy flakes of snow, couldn't see how any order was ever going to come out of such chaos, but it did. Eventually all eleven troops sat their horses in line upon the parade. The four hundred wagons, each drawn by four now docile mules, rumbled into motion, heading south.

Custer, his two staghounds frolicking around him and barking excitedly, bawled an order which was passed down the line of assembled troops. "Left by twos!" The troops surged into motion, forming a column of twos, to the head of which galloped Custer and his staff, followed by the loping staghounds. As he passed General Sheridan's tent, Custer saluted and received Sheridan's salute in return.

The band struck up "The Girl I Left Behind Me," its strains muffled by the sticky flakes of falling snow.

133

Rapidly the column of seven hundred men overtook and passed the slowly moving wagons. Immediately afterward the entire column slowed to a walk, the fastest pace at which the wagon train could travel.

Since Lieutenant Cook's corps of sharpshooters led the column, immediately behind Custer and his staff, it was sometimes possible for Clay Holley to see the colonel and those who rode with him.

Custer wore the buffalo shoes and the fur cap given him by Sheridan and his staff. Holley supposed he also wore the vest, but it was hidden beneath the greatcoat he wore. Besides his staff, with him rode California Joe. Jack Corbin also rode with him, along with other white scouts and eleven Osage trackers with their war chiefs, Little Beaver and Hard Robe. From behind could be heard the muffled cracking of the teamsters' whips as they strove to make the toiling mules maintain the pace of the mounted troops.

Camp Supply disappeared into the driving snow behind. All landmarks disappeared.

Denton rode beside Holley. Daniels and Hines rode immediately ahead. Once or twice Hines turned his head and grinned at Holley and Holley grinned back at him. Snow or no snow, they were on their way. They were headed south. They would find and attack the villages of the hostiles, probably on the banks of the Washita. And, however slight it seemed now, Holley would have his chance. Of finding Julia, Sally, and her son. Of rescuing them, or dying with them, if that was the way it had to be.

134

Half a dozen miles out of Camp Supply the column suddenly halted. With such a long column, it was inevitable that delay in passing the order from unit to unit would result in the units piling up upon each other. Which brought on a lot of sour cursing, complaining, and wondering what the hell was going on.

Lieutenant Cook and his sergeant rode forward to find out what the trouble was. When they came back, Cook explained to the men disgustedly, "Scouts! He's got half a dozen white scouts and eleven Osages and there isn't a goddam one of them that isn't lost! The bastards don't even know what direction we're going."

Clay thought, They ought to be able to tell that by the wind. It had been out of the north all morning and there was no reason to believe that it had changed. One of the men asked, "What the hell are we going to do?"

Cook grinned, his face half-plastered with snow. "Custer's got a compass. He'll keep us heading south."

Slowly, as ponderously as it had halted, the column ground into motion again, with commands echoing and reechoing down the long line which stretched out almost a mile.

Custer ordered Osage flankers out on both sides of the column, sourly wondering aloud whether or not they too would get lost. The unwieldy column ground on. Custer now rode at the very head of it, a compass in hand and partially shielded by the flat of his greatcoat to keep the snow off its face.

Clay Holley hunched down into the collar of his greatcoat. The enlisted men wore fur forage caps instead of the campaign hats worn by the officers. They blew off less readily in the wind, but they provided less protection from the snow. But since the snow was driving at them from behind, their faces were kept relatively clear.

All day long it snowed. At noon Custer halted the column and allowed the men to eat the cold rations that had been issued to them this morning. Most of the men loosened their cinches although few removed their saddles, knowing the horses' backs would only get thoroughly soaked if they did.

After an hour's rest for both horses and men, the column moved on again, floundering aimlessly through the thickening storm, guided only by the compass in Custer's hands.

At dusk they camped. Because of the snow on the ground, they needed no stream to provide them with water. Custer sent California Joe and Jack Corbin out to bring in the Osage flankers. There was little need for it, but he stationed pickets around the entire camp just to be safe.

Clay Holley, Denton, Daniels, and Hines worked together at clearing a space to pitch their tent. They built a huge fire in front of it, and before they ever laid their blankets down, the ground was dry from the fire's warmth.

As darkness fell, the snow slackened, and before they went to sleep, stars were occasionally visible through the overcast sky. Holley said to no one in particular, "Going to be a clear day tomorrow."

Next morning, despite the partial clearing during the night, there was eighteen inches of snow on the ground. Custer had the bugler blow reveille at five, and by the time the sun poked its rim above the horizon the column was once more on the move, needing no compass now.

Custer's staghounds nearly ran themselves to exhaustion chasing rabbits across the unmarked expanse of snow. Finally Custer secured them with ropes and they trotted behind his horse, sides heaving, tongues lolling out, saliva dripping from their jaws.

Holley kept looking for landmarks he might recognize, particularly those that might give him a clue as to whether they were headed toward the place where Tom Denton was buried. But snow had so changed the appearance of the landscape that landmarks that might have been recognizable when the ground was dry now looked entirely different.

The spirits of the men generally were high, despite the discomfort of the deep snow and the difficulty of traveling through it. They shouted, joked, and laughed, and when Custer spotted a small herd of buffalo in the distance and halted the column so that he could pursue them, the men found themselves the highest ground available so they could watch.

Hounds loosed, Custer and two or three of his staff galloped recklessly through the deep snow, heedless of what pitfalls it might conceal, toward the dark shapes of the buffalo.

Occasionally Custer's roaring voice could be heard, calling the staghounds back. He didn't want them running the buffalo before he or the others got close enough to shoot.

Someone said, "Fresh meat tonight, I'll bet."

Holley didn't reply. He could not conceal his utter disgust at the conduct of their commanding officer. To him, if not to Custer, this was a deadly serious business. His wife's life and that of their unborn child were the stakes for which he rode with this column of cavalry. And Sally's life. And Frankie's too.

But to Custer, who was acting more like a boy than a mature man who had held general rank during the war, it was just a lark. He saw Custer and the staghounds catch up with the buffalo, who immediately began to run. Custer sent several of his staff around one side and himself tried to go around the other, to no avail. The huge, powerful beasts were easily able to outdistance the horses in the deep, wet snow.

All except a calf, too short to force a way through the snow. The hounds were on him in a flash, forcing him to turn and face them, with head lowered as if he already had horns and was a match for them.

Holley felt brief sympathy for the calf. The hounds tore at him and, while they kept him occupied, Custer dismounted, floundered through the snow to the beleaguered animal, and with his knife cut the hamstrings. The calf went down.

Custer drove the hounds off with curses and then cut the calf's throat. Standing up, he beckoned, and a couple of men galloped toward him, trailing a packhorse on which to bring in the buffalo calf.

138

A man near Holley said sourly, "The officers' mess will have fresh meat tonight, but we won't, by God."

Holley said, "Isn't enough to go around."

"They could of got one of them big bulls."

"You wouldn't want one of them. It's like eating a pair of boots."

The man subsided, grumbling. Custer and his hounds returned, followed by the two men who had gutted and loaded the calf on the packhorse and were now trailing the packhorse in.

Denton said sourly, "I wonder how much more of this kind of crap there's going to be to slow us down."

"No hurry, Frank. They'll still be there," Holley said.

Frank grumbled, "He's actin' like a goddam kid."

CHAPTER
SIXTEEN

Slowly, all afternoon, the ponderous, unwieldy column ground on southward. Wagons repeatedly got stuck and whenever they did, spare mules would have to be harnessed and hitched ahead of the mules already pulling the stuck wagons to help it out of whatever it had gotten itself mired down in.

There was plenty of rest for the cavalry horses, because they could go no faster than the wagons could. And there was a lot of grumbling among the men, which did nobody any good.

They crossed no Indian trails. Except for the occasional tracks of a band of antelope, a few deer, or buffalo, the white expanse of snow was unmarred. The lack of tracks strengthened Holley's belief that the Indians were already in camp someplace where they would remain until the snow melted and the grass turned green again.

Altogether, they covered less than ten miles that day, but, since the scouts now had their bearings again, the line of travel was reasonably straight and there were no costly time-wasting detours.

That night they camped on one of the south-flowing tributaries of the Canadian. Upon each horse's head was hung a grain morral, and after that, each animal was given enough hay to supplement the ration of oats.

The following day they were once again roused at five, long before dawn, so that they would be ready to move at first light. There was growing impatience in Custer, and in some of his officers, primarily Major Elliott, who seemed very young to Holley to be holding a major's rank. The pair were like hunters on the trail of game, all eagerness and excitement. And, despite his hatred of the Indians for what they had done to him personally, Holley sometimes could not help but think of them as people like himself — men, women, children, oldsters, peacefully camped and waiting for the spring. They had no inkling that Custer's orders ensured the death either by shooting or hanging of every male Indian, the enslavement of every woman and child who escaped the hail of bullets that killed their men.

His own mixed feelings angered him. God knew, he had no reason to waste sympathy on the Indians. And yet the nagging knowledge persisted in him that this land really belonged to the Indians. The atrocities committed by them were in revenge for atrocities earlier committed against them.

Custer had no business here. He had no business searching the Indians out or attacking them. Sherman had sent General Hazen to their agents with funds to support them through the winter. Now Phil Sheridan had sent Custer with orders to kill or hang all warriors found, whether peaceful or otherwise, and to capture and bring in as prisoners all women and children.

141

Then Holley would think of Julia, heavy with their child, in the Indians' hands. He would think of his burned-out home, and of Tom Denton, dead, his wife and child also captives of the Cheyennes. His sympathy for the Indians would then disappear and his hatred would return.

So would his fear. And his feeling of hopelessness. How, in God's name, was he going to find Julia among the hundreds of hide lodges on the banks of the Washita?

On the third day out of Camp Supply the column reached the Canadian River. Normally the Canadian was only a sluggish stream, easily fordable almost anywhere. Now, however, swollen by melting snow and filled with ice and slush, it presented a formidable barrier. The column halted on the high bluff overlooking it. Dismay and irritation were plainly visible not only on Custer's face but in his demeanor and his voice.

Holley, Denton, Hines, and Daniels, near the head of the column of Lieutenant Cook's sharpshooters, could hear Custer's shouting without difficulty. One of the Osage scouts who spoke a little English advised Custer there was a crossing several miles upstream.

Custer asked California Joe and Jack Corbin if the Osage was right. Neither seemed to know. Custer fumed, riding his prancing charger back and forth impatiently, much as a man will pace back and forth while trying to make up his mind. Finally, he himself rode down to the edge of the river and put his own horse into it. The horse immediately sank to his withers in the slush and ice. Custer reined him around and rode back out. He was soaked to his waist but he gave no indication of being cold.

He nodded at Hard Robe. "Go ahead. Take two or three of your Osages with you." Then he looked at young Major Elliott. "Take troops G, H, and M. If you find a crossing that the wagons can negotiate, stay there and send back word."

Elliott saluted. The order to move out rolled down the line. Troops G, H, and M separated themselves from the others and followed Major Elliott, Hard Robe, and the three Osages he had selected to accompany him.

Custer dismounted. He called California Joe, Little Beaver, and the rest of the scouts to him. He had the bugler blow officers' call. The officers of the various units rode forward to join him and the scouts.

Custer, striding back and forth, striking his trousers with his gauntlets, said, "I have no intention of sitting here doing nothing. I want you to spread out and see if you can't find a crossing the wagons can negotiate. Report back to me the instant you find one and I'll come and look at it."

The officers saluted. California Joe, sober for once, and the Osages departed to descend into the canyon of the Canadian to look for a crossing.

Custer continued to stride impatiently back and forth. Holley dismounted and cleared a patch of ground with his foot. He hunkered down comfortably, packed and lighted his pipe. His face was calm, but he was seething inside.

Frank Denton joined him. "I don't see how the hell you can take it like you do. It's your own wife we're going after."

Holley shook his head. "Custer doesn't even know about her. All they're doing is getting you and me safely to where the Indians are. There's no use getting all steamed up. Worry isn't going to accomplish anything."

"Telling Custer might help. If he knew the Indians had three white captives it might make a difference in what he did."

Holley shook his head. "It wouldn't make a damned bit of difference. Not to Custer. He's out to make a hero out of himself and the devil take anyone or anything that stands in the way. We're better off if he doesn't know. That way we'll have a free hand to do what we think is best without any interference from him. I don't want him giving us any direct orders not to interfere."

Denton said grudgingly, "Maybe you're right."

"Besides that, if we tell him, he's going to know us by name, and if we turn up missing later, he's going to be looking for us."

A few of the men broke dead branches off the trees growing in the bed of the river and built small fires in places they had previously cleared of snow. California Joe and the Osages were gone for nearly an hour. When they returned, however, they had news for Custer that there was a crossing about a mile downstream.

"Can the wagons get down into the riverbed, across the river, and then up out of the riverbed on the other side?" Custer asked California Joe.

"I think so. But it'll take more'n four mules to pull them across the river and up out of the riverbed. It'll take eight, at least, but it ain't something that can't be done."

Custer glanced briefly at his hunting-case watch, obviously trying to decide whether there would be time for that kind of crossing effort before dark overtook them. Apparently he decided there would, because he ordered the column forward, riding himself with California Joe and the Osage scouts.

The mounted troopers reached the spot in less than half an hour. Custer rode down the steep trail after the scouts to the river and sat his horse on the bank staring at it while the four troops of cavalry watched from above.

At this spot, the riverbed was nearly double its normal width as it made a sharp bend and then straightened out. The cutbank on the near side was steep and rough, but there was a gentle grade ascending on the other side. A few cottonwoods and willows blocked the trail on the other side, and Custer immediately issued orders for them to be felled and dragged out of the way.

By the time that had been accomplished, the first of the wagons rumbled into view. Custer himself climbed to the seat of the first wagon to attempt the descent. The regular driver manned the heavy iron brake handle which, when pulled back, activated a brake beam which pressed a shoe against each rear wheel. A cottonwood log was chained to the rear axle of the wagon to provide additional braking on the steep slope. The teamster suggested chaining the rear wheels as well, but Custer was in too much of a hurry and decided against doing that.

The heavy wagon tipped and nearly overturned as it started down the slope, but under Custer's deft handling it righted itself and lumbered on down the slope, wheels skidding, cottonwood log mostly dragging but sometimes rolling and nearly overtaking the wagon it was supposed to be holding back.

There wasn't a man watching who didn't draw a long breath of relief when the wagon reached the bottom of the slope. Two teams of mules, which had been driven down the slope immediately in the wagon's wake, were now hitched ahead of the four mules already pulling it. The log was unchained from the wagon's rear. Custer climbed down, mounted his horse, which had been brought to him, and led the way across the slush- and ice-choked river. The scouts had been right. It was no more than three feet deep in any spot, and mostly less than two. The wagon crossed it easily, and also negotiated the slope beyond that climbed up out of the riverbed.

Already the second wagon was on its way down, and as soon as it reached the bottom, a third started down. Dismounted troopers toiled and sweated, chaining and unchaining braking logs, dragging them back up the slope, hitching extra mules to the wagons starting up and unhitching them from wagons which had already reached the safety of the level plain on the other side.

Hour after hour passed. Three wagons capsized and had to be righted with much effort and wasted time.

Custer kept looking impatiently at his watch, and kept glancing upstream in the direction Elliott and his three troops had gone.

The sun sank slowly down the western sky, unnoticed by Clay Holley, who was working and who was soaked with sweat despite the chilly air and the soggy snow and mud underfoot.

By the time a hundred wagons had crossed, the trail both down and up was completely cleared of snow and had been turned into a mud slide in which it was difficult to control a wagon at all. Now, despite Custer's reluctance, it was necessary to chain the rear wheels and also necessary to chain two logs behind each wagon instead of one. Watching one of the heavily loaded wagons make the descent was a hair-raising experience. Holley, grinning faintly, noticed several times how white the teamsters' faces were when they reached the bottom of the grade.

For the first time since Julia had been kidnapped by the Indians, Holley worked so hard that he temporarily forgot about her, forgot why he was here, forgot that she was in the hands of the Indians.

Afterward, when the last wagon had finally climbed out on the other side, when the supplies in two wrecked, wagons had been laboriously carried up and reloaded into other wagons, he paused and again remembered her and was ashamed that, even for a moment, he had forgotten her.

And yet he felt better, despite his near exhaustion, than he had for a long, long time. He realized one thing he hadn't realized before. He had brooded too long and too much over something that could not be changed.

He had told Denton that worry didn't help. The trouble was, he hadn't been following his own advice.

When the time finally came, if it did, when he had another chance to rescue Julia, Sally, and the boy, his mind ought to be clear, able to think and plan, to make logical, right decisions, not clouded or influenced by earlier worry about all the things that might go wrong.

Suddenly Holley saw Custer stiffen and stand in his stirrups, staring northward in the direction Elliott and his three troops had gone. He saw a rider coming, pushing hard.

The rider was on the south side of the Canadian and was almost immediately recognizable as Jack Corbin, the white scout who had accompanied Elliott.

He pulled his lathered, plunging horse to a halt in front of Custer. "Major Elliott has found an Indian trail, a big one, General, and he's following it!"

Custer's face lighted with a kind of wild excitement. At last he had his Indian trail. Fame, Glory, and Vindication awaited him at the end of it.

CHAPTER
SEVENTEEN

No longer, now, was there indolence or inattention among the troopers assembled here on the south bank of the Canadian. Tired they might be from the day's extremely heavy work getting the four hundred supply wagons across the Canadian. But news of a fresh Indian trail and the certainty that Custer would follow it stimulated all of them, including Clay Holley and the three who had pledged themselves to him.

Custer bawled, "Someone bring Corbin a fresh horse!"

A dozen men rode forward to proffer their horses to the scout. He selected one after looking carefully at them all. He mounted and glanced questioningly at the general.

"Intercept Major Elliott. Tell him to follow the hostiles trail until eight. Then have him stop and rest his horses and his men. Tell him we will join him at the earliest and take up the pursuit again."

Ordinarily pursuing a hostile trail in the dark would have been virtually impossible. But with still more than a foot of snow on the ground, it presented no difficulty at all.

149

Clay thought wryly that not once had Custer given any consideration to his men or to their mounts. They had ridden and toiled all day, with never more than a few minutes rest at most. Now they were off to pick up an Indian Trail and would ride all night and all day tomorrow if necessary. And when they finally caught up with their prey, they would fight. No matter how exhausted. No matter how hungry, they would fight.

Corbin galloped away on the borrowed horse. Custer shouted, "Bugler! Sound officers' call!"

The clear notes of officers' call floated out over the deep canyon of the Canadian. Officers from the various troops rode forward to join the general. Clay Holley and his three companions edged their horses closer so that they could hear.

Crisply, with his extreme self-assurance only partially masking his excitement, Custer said, "Gentlemen, we will leave the main body of the supply train here. I want only seven wagons and an ambulance, to be under the command of Quartermaster Captain Bell. Captain Bell, you will see to it that the seven wagons are carrying the things we are going to need. Ammunition, lots of it. Rations. Grain and hay for the horses. Extra horseshoes and the equipment the farriers will need for replacing shoes that have been thrown. No tents. No blankets. Gentlemen, we are going to fight before we sleep again!"

A few men cheered. A few more cursed their commander sourly. Custer roared, as his officers rode away toward their respective commands. "Twenty

150

minutes. We leave in twenty minutes and God help the man who isn't ready by then to ride!"

Captain Bell lingered. "What about the rest of the wagon train, General?"

"They are to follow, with an escort of eighty men, mounted on the most nearly spent of the horses. The officer of the day will be in command."

Fifty feet away, one of Custer's officers suddenly reined his horse around. He rode back to Custer and saluted as he stopped his horse. Holley recognized him as Captain Louis Hamilton, whose troop, due to his untiring efforts, was one of the best in the regiment. He said, "General, I am officer of the day."

Custer said, "I am perfectly aware of that fact, Captain Hamilton."

"General, for God's sake, don't leave me behind!"

"Somebody has to stay behind, Captain Hamilton. You are one of my best officers. With the supply train in your charge, I will not have to worry about its safety."

"General . . ."

"Captain Hamilton!" It was a dismissal, an order to stop the argument.

But Hamilton was not to be denied. "General, my troop is one of the best in the regiment, as you well know."

Custer stared coldly at him.

"General, I deserve the chance to lead them into battle."

"Goddammit, Captain Hamilton, you have my orders!" Custer was furious and it showed.

151

Hamilton apparently recognized the futility of pursuing the subject further. He saluted angrily and reined his horse away.

Holley felt sorry for the man. But he was busy getting his own horse ready for the march. One by one, he carefully inspected the horse's feet, scraping off the caked mud and frozen snow so that he could see the condition both of the shoe and of the hoof as well.

With that done, he unsaddled, and with an empty grain sack from one of the wagons carrying grain he briskly rubbed the horse's back until it was almost completely dry. He shook out the damp saddle blanket, placed it carefully on the horse's back, making certain there were no wrinkles in it and that it fitted smoothly.

The saddle went on next, and he cinched it down. Lastly, he put a measure of oats into a morral, removed the bit from his horse's mouth, and hung the morral over his head. While the horse was eating, he went around to the far side of the grain wagon and put twenty or thirty pounds of oats into the sack. Returning, he secured it behind his saddle, covering it with his slicker so that it would not be seen. Denton, Hines, and Daniels, seeing what he had done, followed suit, surreptitiously and without getting caught. All knew that the demands they would place on their horses might far exceed those placed on the mounts of the other members of the regiment.

Rations for themselves were another matter. They would be issued rations as long as they were with the regiment. When they separated themselves from it, they could either live off the country or rely on dried meat and berries obtained from the tipis of the Indians.

Fifteen of the twenty allotted minutes had passed when Captain Hamilton returned, with Lieutenant Mathey following along in his wake, rubbing his eyes as if he could hardly see.

Custer looked impatiently at Hamilton. "What now?"

Hamilton's voice broke when he replied, "General, I've got to go with my men. Lieutenant Mathey is snowblind and won't be able to go along anyway. General, please, let him take my place with the supply train. He's perfectly willing. Riding with the sun on the snow will be torture for him."

Custer stared at Mathey, who tried to return his glance through eyes swimming with tears. "Is that right, Lieutenant? Are you willing to take Captain Hamilton's place?"

Mathey nodded. "Yes, sir."

"And do you think you can do the job?"

"Sir, I have never failed to do a job assigned to me."

Custer nodded. "All right. The supply train is in your charge, Lieutenant. But I want you to bear in mind that, by destroying our supplies, the Indians could make things very difficult."

"Yes, sir. I'll have eighty troopers. The supplies will be available when you need them, General."

Hamilton was grinning from ear to ear. He looked as if he'd like to shout with glee, or embrace Custer, or both. He controlled himself however, thanked Custer fervently, saluted, and took his leave. Mathey followed more slowly, trying to shield his eyes from the light.

The twenty minutes were, by now, nearly up. Custer dragged his big hunting-case watch from his pocket, opened it, and looked at the face. To his adjutant he said, "Move them out."

Orders were bellowed and repeated, and repeated again. The command, except for the supply train and the eighty troopers assigned to escort it, formed and, led by Custer, California Joe, and the remaining Osages, took the trail left in the snow by Jack Corbin returning to relay Custer's orders to Major Elliott.

The trail took a diagonal southwestward, not toward the place Elliott had been when he sent Corbin with his report but toward the spot it was estimated he would be by the time Custer and his remaining troops reached him. The plan was to cut his trail and then follow it to where he had camped.

Behind the column, which was traveling at a steady trot, the huge supply train lumbered into motion. Ahead of it rode a score of mounted troopers and behind it a like amount. Flankers were out on both sides. Each wagon carried a teamster and a helper, armed with a Spencer carbine. Holley didn't think there was much likelihood that the wagon train would be either attacked or destroyed, mainly because the Indians didn't even know that it was here.

The trail found by Elliott must have been made by one of the last groups of Indians to leave Kansas and head for their traditional winter camp in Indian Territory.

154

The sun sank in a cloudless western sky. As it set, it cast a bronze sheen over the vast expanse of snow which had, during the warm day, thawed enough on the surface to give it a glossy appearance that caught and reflected the rays of the dying sun.

Holley watched his mount carefully, looking for signs of faltering. All day they had traveled through snow, slush, and mud. Countless times, Holley had been called upon to ride back and forth across the Canadian River crossing to assist in some way one of the wagons of the huge supply train.

The horses needed rest. All the horses needed rest. But they weren't going to get very much of it. Not tonight at least. Perhaps, if Custer did not find the Indian camp he was looking for by daylight tomorrow, he would take a few hours to rest the horses and the men.

Holley knew how much depended on the strength of his horse when the crucial moment came. He wished there was some way he could save the animal's strength now but he knew that there was not.

The sun disappeared, along with the orange glow it cast above the horizon. Gray dusk came down across the vast and empty land. The column ground on, stringing out a little now.

Denton rode beside Holley. Daniels and Hines were immediately behind. The four men closed up enough so that they could talk without being overheard by either the pair ahead or the pair behind.

Hines asked, "What's the plan?"

Holley said helplessly, "I haven't got a plan. We don't even know how many Indians Elliott is following. We don't know the size of the encampment they're going to lead us to or even if it is the right one. I haven't the slightest idea how I'm going to find my wife in any case. But I know her pretty well and she's nobody's fool. If she's here and if there's a way of letting us know where she is, which lodge she's in, she'll find it. And she'll stay out of sight so she doesn't get herself shot. At least that's what I'm counting on."

Hines said, "By now, she'll likely be dressed like a squaw, so she'd better stay out of sight. I don't figure this bunch is going to care much who they shoot."

Holley thought about the unhesitating way Daniels and Hines had offered their help, which they knew involved the risk of prison if they deserted and were caught. They had asked nothing in return, expected nothing. After his experiences in Dodge City with bankers, cattle buyers, and potential Indian fighters, the simple generosity of their action made his throat feel tight. He said, "I want you two to know that if you're interested in a cattle job after this is over with, you've got one for as long as you live."

The remark seemed to embarrass both Daniels and Hines. They dropped back. Holley glanced aside at Frank Denton. "You'll likely be running your brother's place for Sally and her son."

"Likely will."

Holley realized he was assuming they would rescue Julia, Sally, and her son, that none of them would be killed in the process, and that they would get safely away. He knew such an assumption was stupid. It was impossible, under the conditions he knew would exist.

He made himself put aside his gloomy thoughts. Darkness succeeded dusk, but with the white cover of snow on the ground it never got completely dark. Each man could still see the pair riding ahead of him.

After traveling at a trot for about half an hour, Custer slowed to let the seven supply wagons and the ambulance catch up. Holley grinned to himself in the darkness, thinking how Custer would be fretting now. He had a trail, a fresh one. There was no chance on earth of losing it.

The fight he wanted so desperately was now within his grasp. And he had both the troops and the firepower to emerge victorious.

At last, about an hour after dark, they cut the trail left by Major Elliott and his three troops. They immediately turned into it, and a couple of hours later brought Elliott's bivouac into sight.

Elliott was camped on the bank of a small stream. He had permitted small fires to be lighted. There was much shouting back and forth between the men of Elliott's command and those of Custer's.

Custer passed the word that there would be a two-hour halt. Horses were to be unsaddled and fed both grain and hay and their backs rubbed down. After that, the men could build small fires, make coffee and cook bacon and fry hardtack in the grease.

A jubilant but impatient Custer paced back and forth and back and forth, while his charger was cared for, while a meal was prepared and brought to him. On his face was the vision of glory that was living in his heart. He was like a hound on a leash, waiting to be released.

CHAPTER
EIGHTEEN

From Custer's point of view, the next two hours must have seemed an eternity. But in the weary troopers' view, the time was all too short. A partial moon had risen and it cast abundant light over the snowy landscape.

Fires were killed. Each troop was formed into a column of twos. By now, a crust had formed on the top of the snow, and with each step taken by man or horse, it broke and crunched noisily. Therefore, when the column moved out, Hard Robe and Little Beaver went ahead on foot. A couple of hundred yards back, close enough to keep their dark figures in view, came Custer, mounted, and the rest of the scouts, including Jack Corbin and California Joe. Half a mile behind Custer and the scouts, the rest of the column came, kept back that far lest the crunching of the horses' hoofs through the crusted snow be heard by the "enemy" they pursued.

Custer knew he was pursuing Indians but he had no idea what Indians. He had no idea to which tribe they belonged. He had no idea whether they were hostile or friendly. He had no idea where they had come from or

159

where they were going. To him they were only the "enemy" or his "quarry."

Hard Robe and Little Beaver had told Custer the trail was fresh, made sometime today. They were moving down a long, shallow grade now, into the valley of the Washita, some eighty miles west of Fort Cobb, where General Hazen, serving temporarily as agent, was trying under the terms of the Medicine Lodge Treaty of 1867, to care for his Indian charges with the limited amount of money given him by the government.

Elliott, riding with Lieutenant Cook at the head of Cook's sharpshooter corps, was almost beside himself with excitement. But in Holley it was not excitement that kept rising. It was dread. What if this excited, blood-hungry army killed everyone and everything in sight? What if Julia and Sally were in the camp and failed either to hide or to make it plain that they were white? Once more he wished desperately that he had been able to raise a private army of civilians to go after them. At least then he would have been in control. His "army" would not have been under the command of a half-mad glory hunter interested only in brightening his tarnished reputation with an impressive "victory."

But even if he *had* been able to raise a private army, there was no assurance it could have succeeded. Instead of seven hundred men, he would have had fewer than fifty. And it was certain there were hundreds, maybe thousands of Indians camped along the Washita.

For several hours, they traveled steadily. The wagons and the ambulance, which had caught up during the

160

two-hour rest, now labored along half a mile behind the troopers, losing ground steadily because the mules were tired.

At last Hard Robe and Little Beaver stopped and stood utterly still for several moments. Then Hard Robe turned and came trotting back to where Custer was. In his broken English he informed Custer that they had smelled smoke. They knew the quarry was very near.

Custer motioned him on, cautioning him to be very careful. He didn't want the Indians alerted to his presence, for that would spoil his plan.

Hard Robe returned to Little Beaver and, slowly and cautiously, they continued. A little later Hard Robe returned to Custer a second time. "Find fire, built yesterday. Find second fire, built today. Herd boys build it mebbe."

Once more Custer motioned him on, cautioning him to even greater care. At last, below the crest of a long rise, both Osages stopped. This time it was Little Beaver who came creeping back. "Big camp other side of hill. Come see."

Custer ordered everyone to remain in place. He himself dismounted and accompanied Little Beaver to where Hard Robe waited in the snow.

Holley watched without being able to make out what was going on. He realized that he was sweating, despite the chill of the night air. He realized that his hands were shaking and he had to press his knees hard against his horse's sides to keep them from trembling.

To those with him, he said, "When we attack, look for something, anything, that will let us know where they are. A petticoat scrap on a lodgepole. Anything. I don't know if she's here but if she is I damn well know she'll do something."

"You don't think Custer intends to attack at night?"

Holley shook his head. "He told Sheridan it was going to be a surround. Huh-uh, he'll spend what's left of the night positioning the troops. Then when it gets light and the Indians are still asleep, he'll attack. Just like Chivington did at Sand Creek four years ago."

Custer was now down on hands and knees, crawling through the crusted snow toward the top of the shallow rise.

Reaching it, all three men stopped, lying prone and motionless in the snow. Below him, Custer saw the shimmer of moonlight upon a winding river that had to be the Washita. Beyond, he saw dark masses that he judged to be trees. Closer, he saw the sluggish movement of animals, probably the pony herd. So vast was this mass of animals that he guessed there must be between five hundred and a thousand of them. They had apparently long since pawed the snow away from the grass beneath and were now grazing peacefully. A herd bell tinkled, and distantly a dog barked.

On this side of the river, now that his eyes were becoming accustomed to the scene, Custer could now see the shine of moonlight upon the conical shapes of tipis. Hundreds of them. They stretched away to right and left until they disappeared into infinity.

Most of the fires were out because it was early morning now and nearly all the Indians were asleep.

Custer whispered to Hard Robe, "Do you think they have sentries out?"

Hard Robe shook his head. "Feel safe. No need for guards. Camped near Agency. Promised everything be all right."

The smell of smoke drifted toward them on the light night breeze. Custer touched both scouts and began his withdrawal from the hill. He had seen what he had to see. Lying there, he had formed his battle plan.

He reached the spot where he had left Corbin, California Joe, and the other Osage scouts. To Corbin he said, "Ride back along the line. Tell all my officers to gather here at once."

Corbin rode away. Hard Robe said, "General, no good to attack. Too many Indians. Too much spread out. We only see part of horse herd they got."

California Joe, having been nipping on his whiskey-filled canteen and perhaps reckless because of it said, "Ain't these the Indians General Hazen is supposed to be feedin' and takin' care for the winter?"

Custer said shortly, "Are you questioning my judgment? We followed a trail here, a trail that came south across the Kansas line. These are the same hostiles that have been harassing us all summer. Only now that the grass is covered and game is short, they want to camp peacefully and be fed by the government. Well, to hell with them. We will attack at dawn."

Cook's sharpshooter corps had been moving closer, and now Holley heard those last impassioned words. He hoped fervently that Julia would have time tomorrow in some way to let her presence be known.

Before she was cut down by the hail of bullets along with all the Indians.

The snow around the village where Julia Holley, Sally Denton, and Sally's boy, Frankie, were had been tramped down by the Indians who lived in the lodges there and by their horses and their visitors until it was nearly gone in some places, polished to an icy glaze in others.

Julia still watched the horizons to the north off and on all during the daylight hours though she knew there was little chance she would see anything. Yet she also knew that if she ever abandoned hope, then life would lose its value and she would no longer care whether she lived or died. The prospect of spending the remainder of her life with these Indians was intolerable. The brave who had taken her as wife had two other wives and they never missed a chance to strike her; they gave her the most unpleasant and heaviest work to do. They showed her nothing but dislike and contempt.

But it was Sally who disturbed her the most. Sally had been raped repeatedly by the braves of the party that had captured them. Afterward she had been taken as squaw by the brave who had originally seized her outside the house. He had taken her into his tipi along with his other, Indian wife.

It was the expression, or lack of it, in Sally's face, that disturbed Julia the most. And Sally neglected Frankie, who, however, seemed to have adapted better to the new environment than either of the women had. Dressed like any Indian child he played with others of his age and seemed to have forgotten the trauma of his capture and that of his mother and Julia.

Julia herself grew heavier with her child, and every day she thanked God she was carrying him. He had kept her from the abuse of her Indian captors. He had kept her from any demands that might have been made upon her by the Indian who had taken her as his third wife.

Once, a delegation from the Indian Agency at Fort Cobb visited the village, and when they came into sight, she, Sally, and Frankie were quickly hustled inside so that they would not be seen.

That they weren't seen by the agency employees was disturbing but not devastating because Julia knew her husband Clay. She knew him to be strong, determined, and not a man to quit at anything. He would come again. How, she couldn't know. She only knew that he would come.

She also knew the difficulties he would face in finding her. There must be hundreds of hide lodges up and down this section of the Washita. How was he going to know which of them sheltered her? It therefore became important to her that she devise some plan of letting him know, when the time came, where she was.

She still had a petticoat, which she wore beneath the buckskin Indian woman's dress that had been given her. It was the only thing she had that he would recognize.

But he couldn't recognize it unless it was clearly visible. And the only place it might be clearly visible was at the peak of the tipi.

A tipi is constructed of a number of long pine poles. Their heavy ends are usually placed either in shallow holes or a shallow ditch to hold them in place. The upper ends are lashed together with rawhide. The tipi itself, made of buffalo hides sewed together with rawhide strips, is stretched over the framework thus formed. Julia had to find a way to hoist her petticoat to the peak of the tipi so that it could be seen.

There were two other poles that reached from the ground to the tipi top. These were each secured to the ends of a smoke flap so that the flaps could be adjusted according to the wind direction and smoke generated by the fire in the center of the tipi floor would be drawn out by the wind rather than blown back in.

Julia managed to steal the tanned hide of a buffalo calf. Carefully, whenever she was alone, she cut the hide into a long, continuous strip laboriously with a knife, starting at the outside and working in toward the center in a circular movement until at last she had a half-inch-wide strip of strong, tough buffalo hide more than long enough to reach to the top of the pole and back to the ground again.

The second part of the task was more demanding. She had to take down one of the smoke-flap poles when nobody was around or when everyone was asleep. She chose to do it when everyone was asleep, in the middle of the night. Having done it, she tied a loop of rawhide to the top of the pole and ran her strip of tanned buffalo hide through the loop. Then, with great difficulty and with much strain to her strength, she replaced the pole. She wound the strips of buffalo hide around the pole and secured them as high as she could reach, hoping they would not be noticed by whoever adjusted the smoke flaps from now on.

Silently she crept back to her bed of buffalo robes. She felt both hopeful and elated. She now had the means with which to let Clay know where she was. She could tie her petticoat or a part of it to the strip of buffalo hide and hoist it to the tip of the smoke-flap pole, where it would stand out like a sore thumb. After that, she need only hide herself within the tipi and wait for him to come for her. She would be safe, unless a bullet, randomly fired, came through the buffalo-hide tipi and struck her by accident.

Now she prayed that nobody would notice the buffalo hide strip wound around the pole and reaching to its top. Worrying, she slept not at all that night.

CHAPTER
NINETEEN

Holley had supposed, as most of the other men probably had, that Custer, having been the youngest brigadier general in the Northern Army during the war, would be a master of cavalry tactics. He therefore found it incredible that Custer would make his battle plans without first ordering a thorough reconnaissance of the Indian villages he intended to attack. Custer had lain at the crest of that little knoll and had seen horses and hide tipis in the valley of the Washita. In the darkness he could have formed no accurate estimate as to their numbers or extent. But like many another cavalry commander, he had nothing but contempt for the Indians' fighting abilities despite the way they had succeeded in making fools of the Army near Fort Dodge during the summer months.

With Holley and perhaps half of Cook's company of sharpshooters close enough to hear, Custer issued orders to his commanders. "Elliott, you are to take troops G, H, and M, circle wide to the left, and, when daylight comes, attack from the left rear.

"Captain Thompson, you will take troops B and F, circle to the right, and, when daylight comes attack from the right rear. Captain Myers, you will command

E and I. Captain Hamilton, you will take troops A and C. And, Captain West, you will take troops D and K. All six troops will attack from this side, along with Lieutenant Cook and his sharpshooter corps.

"Major Elliott will be in overall command of the force attacking from the other side. I will command the force attacking from this side. The plan, Major, is that we will attack first from this side. We will drive the hostiles toward you and you should be able to prevent any from making their escape. My orders from General Sheridan were to kill or hang all adult males. Naturally, if we kill most of them with bullets there will be fewer hangings to occupy our time. Am I understood?"

He had just issued a license for the men indiscriminately to slaughter everything that moved. Holley wanted to shout a protest, to tell Custer and his officers that two white women and a white boy might be down there somewhere with the Indians. He didn't because he knew it would do no good. It would only draw the attention of all officers and noncoms to him and make him subject to their scrutiny throughout the battle. Besides, nothing would be changed. The orders had been issued.

Custer asked, "Any questions?"

There were none. Custer ordered California Joe and two of the Osages to accompany Elliott. He sent Jack Corbin and two more of the Osages along with Thompson to the right, keeping Hard Robe, Little Beaver, and the remaining Osages with him.

Elliott and his three troops moved off toward the left, staying well behind the crest of the ridge and

169

disappeared into the distance. Thompson took his two troops away to the right, also staying well back from the crest of the ridge and moving at a walk so as to make less noise.

Custer sent Myers with Troops E and I to the left with orders to spread out his line about a quarter mile away. He sent Hamilton with troops A and C to the right with similar orders. West with troops D and K and Lieutenant Cook with his sharpshooter corps he spread out from their present location until the line thus formed was nearly half a mile long.

Everything was now in readiness. Accompanied by Little Beaver and Hard Robe, Custer once more crept to the crest of the ridge from which he could look down into the Indian camp.

Cautioned by their officers to rest but to make no noise, the men conversed in whispers or lowered tones. Holley looked at the eastern horizon at least a dozen times every fifteen minutes, searching for that telltale streak of gray that would announce the coming of the dawn.

He gathered Denton, Hines, and Daniels around him and moved far enough away from the others so that they would not be overheard. He said, "Stay together. If I take off away from the others, stay with me even if Cook or any of the noncoms yells at us to come back. I'm not going to get hung up in one place while my wife is dying someplace else."

The other men grunted their assent. Holley thought of Julia, perhaps no more than half a mile away from him right now. How was she? Had they mistreated her?

170

Did she still have her child safely inside of her, or had beatings and other maltreatment caused her to lose the child? Or was she dead?

All were questions that had no answers but that still tormented him. The thought of her possibly being so close yet so impossibly beyond his reach nearly drove him out of his mind. The thought that he might find her killed by the Indians because of the attack or by one of the wildly fired bullets of the troopers was even worse. Yet he told himself that he had done — that he was doing — all that was humanly possible.

So he watched for the streak of gray in the east, both anxious for it and dreading it.

It appeared at last, seeming to be an illusion, but growing lighter and lighter with each passing moment. He could feel the change in the men around him and that change communicated itself to the horses too.

Cinches, which had been loosened during the wait, were tightened in preparation. Men checked the ammunition in their belt pouches for the tenth time, and rechecked the loads in their Spencer carbines once more.

Custer was now pacing back and forth like a caged lion. The battle for which he had yearned during his long year of suspension was about to start. Vindication was at hand. Glory awaited him over the crest of this shallow ridge. Holley wondered if he bothered to think that some of his men, his own men, were going to die as were the Indians. He wondered if any commander, of any army, thinks about casualties at the moment of battle, or whether his head is filled only with strategy and his worry reserved for the possibility that he might lose.

At last, when the light was strong enough to pick out individual, scrubby pines at the crest of the ridge several hundred yards away, Custer beckoned the trooper who was holding his horse. He took the reins and swung to the saddle. He drew his saber and raised it high above his head.

For a moment he sat there, poised and motionless, as if some photographer were committing his dashing figure to film for all posterity. Then he waved his saber forward and shouted, "Bugler, sound the charge!"

The clear notes of the charge cut through the silence of the frosty morning air, probably muffled from the Indian villages down below because of the intervening ridge, but clearly heard by the sharpshooters of Lieutenant Cook and by the troopers of West's D and K. The buglers of the troops under Myers and Hamilton also sounded the charge, faintly heard by Clay Holley almost as an echo of the first bugle call.

As the band struck up "Garry Owen," the line surged into movement, Custer, Cook, and West taking their commands ahead at a walk to allow time for the others to hear and pass on the command and to reach the crest of the ridge at the same time Custer did.

It was light enough now to see the length of the entire line. It undulated like a serpent, but was fairly straight before it reached the crest of the ridge. Custer, unable to contain himself any longer, kicked his charger in the ribs and made him trot, and as soon as the entire line had also reached that gait, kicked his horse again, now letting loose a wild yell.

The yell was taken up by the men both ways along the galloping, undulating line. From some of the men, the yell was only a wordless shout; in some it was a kind of screech. From a few, who had served the South during the war, it was the bloodcurdling Rebel yell that had sent Union troops fleeing from many an entrenched position by its awesome intensity.

They swept across the crest of the ridge at a hard gallop, the hoofs of their horses throwing up great gobs of snow and mud. The Indian horse herd, grazing peacefully between them and the Indian villages, fled in panic, stampeding straight toward the villages. Custer yelled again, waving his saber, and Holley got a glimpse of his face from less than twenty-five yards away.

It was taut with excitement. The lips were parted to reveal the teeth. The eyes had a burning quality, as if to Custer this was the ultimate in all human experience.

Then Holley pulled his glance from that of his commander, and looked ahead with frantic desperation. The Indian ponies had reached the edge of the first of the villages. Massed and bunched, almost shoulder to shoulder, the stampeding horses went through and over the hide tipis, tangling themselves in rawhide thongs, falling, shrilly neighing, and all fighting to free themselves and to get on through.

Frantically, desperately, Holley looked to right and left, searching for any sign that would tell him where Julia was. He saw nothing and he knew that the villages had probably been caught too much by surprise for Julia to have hoisted anything.

Indians came running from the tipis left standing, or crawling from those that had been flattened by the stampeding horses, all in various stages of undress. Most of the men wore only breechclouts. Women, for the most part, had only blankets or buffalo robes clutched around them against the cold.

And now, within rifle range, Custer bellowed, "Commence firing!"

All along the galloping line the Spencers crackled. Women, children, unarmed men went down, some of them immediately staining the whiteness of the snow with the redness of their blood. Dogs fled in panic, yipping whether or not they had been hit.

Holley had no way of knowing it, but this particular village was that of Black Kettle, the peacemaker among the Cheyennes, whose village had also been the one attacked by Chivington at Sand Creek. Then, as now, he had been promised the protection of the government and of the U. S. Army, and both times he had been betrayed. He was one of the first to die. But had Holley known, he would not have cared.

Now the line of screeching cavalrymen swept on into the shambles the pony herd had left of the villages. Custer's saber slashed, already red with blood. Spencers, emptied on the first wild charge, now were used as clubs. Holley could see no distinction between the treatment accorded men and women, and he saw a number of screaming tiny children trampled under the horses' hoofs.

Still he was looking, even as the fleeing Indians splashed into the river and across. The galloping troopers under Elliott were coming now, shooting, slashing, and clubbing the terrified survivors of Custer's attack upon the villages. For a few moments the stampeding Indian pony herd caused confusion among Elliott's men as they tried to break on through the line, but finally they turned aside and galloped away parallel to the stream toward the north and west.

Holley looked around for the men who had sworn to help him rescue his wife. Denton was almost immediately beside him and his face was red with fury. He bawled, "If they were there, they sure ain't there any more!"

Beyond him Holley saw Hines and Daniels, and he yelled, "Stay with me! There's villages all up and down this stream. We haven't hit half of them!"

That was the truth. The Indian villages must have stretched along the banks of the Washita for several miles. The charge had cut out a swath in the center perhaps a mile or a mile and a half long. And now Custer seemed to become aware of the fact, seemed to become aware that he had wiped out less than half of the total Indian encampment he had attacked.

Elliott's command by now was on the far side of the Washita, mopping up Indians trying to escape. Many of Custer's men had dismounted and were going through the tipis left standing, looking for loot. Occasionally a shot would sound from inside one of the hide lodges, meaning either that some Indian had been shot or that a trooper had.

Completely routed, wakened by that bloodcurdling yell from the attacking troops, and for the most part unable to reach their weapons, these Indians were utterly defeated before the troops under Custer and those commanded by Elliott met on the far bank of the Washita.

But from a group of fifteen or twenty tipis untouched either by the stampeding pony herd or by the subsequent cavalry charge, on Custer's left, a group of Cheyenne warriors now appeared, armed, some partially dressed, and herding their women and children into the brush that lined the riverbank, pushing them downstream toward the southeast and safety.

The men themselves, forty or fifty in number, turned, once their women and children had disappeared, and faced Custer's cavalry, now milling among the smashed and emptied lodges they had first attacked.

Elliott, his boyish face glowing with excitement, raised his saber and waved it toward the group of Cheyennes. "Here's for a brevet or a coffin!" he shouted melodramatically. "Who'll come with me?"

Holley didn't know whether Custer would have stopped him or not if he'd been close enough. A dozen or more men, as excited as Elliott, reined their horses over and spurred to join him.

And suddenly Holley saw the thing he had been looking for, beyond the mass of Cheyenne fighting men, less than a quarter mile downstream. It was a large piece of cloth looking white at this distance, fluttering from the smoke pole of a lodge.

To Denton and Hines and Daniels he roared, "There it is!"

They needed no urging. As he galloped his horse recklessly after Elliott, Holley could hear them pounding along behind.

The Cheyennes, who had briefly massed to protect their fleeing women and children now turned and ran themselves. And Elliott, all restraint gone, galloped after them, followed by a total of nineteen men, counting Holley and the three who had pledged their help to him.

CHAPTER
TWENTY

Custer was at least two hundred yards from Major Elliott when Elliott yelled and galloped in pursuit of the retreating Indians. He opened his mouth to order Elliott back, then closed it without saying anything, knowing Elliott probably couldn't hear him in all the uproar and probably wouldn't heed him if he did.

Glancing around, he could see that he had achieved his purpose. He had his victory, an overwhelming and decisive one. At least fifty tipis had been brought down, or vacated. Their occupants lay everywhere, mostly dead, a few wounded. A small handful of squaws with children stood huddled in a group, their hands upraised in surrender. Custer spotted one who was strikingly beautiful and made up his mind that later, when there was time, he would seek that one out. He had not seen his wife for weeks.

To the bugler, sitting his horse less than a dozen yards away, Custer shouted, "Sound officers' call."

The bugler immediately sounded the call. From all directions the various officers rode toward their commander. Captain Hamilton did not appear. He had been the first of Custer's men to die, shot through the heart.

Custer roared his orders, "Mop up whatever survivors there are in this immediate vicinity, but stay alert for attack from the other villages!"

Commanders gathered their troops, re-forming them into some semblance of order. Methodically they worked their way through the trees and brush, killing every Indian who resisted, taking as prisoners those who did not. Custer ordered the tipis torn down. One tipi was to be packed upon a travois as a souvenir for himself. He ordered the rest placed in a huge pile, along with all of the Indians' household goods. The entire pile was to be set ablaze. The buffalo hide, the dried meat, and grease would burn with a hot flame and send up a towering pillar of dense black smoke.

Custer ordered that the Indian pony herd, which had halted in the trees below the village, be rounded up, brought back, and held in place for disposal later when there was more time.

From downstream, in the direction Elliott and his nineteen men had gone, a few crackling shots were heard, sounding like strings of firecrackers being exploded on the Fourth of July.

Mounted Indians, fully dressed and armed, now appeared on the bluffs overlooking the ravaged and destroyed villages. The seven-vehicle wagon train and the ambulance, left behind during the swift night march, caught up, and the troopers accompanying it began firing aimlessly at these Indians, who were well out of range.

Slowly, slowly, the din of battle faded. Few arrows now came whistling into the troopers' ranks. Fewer and

179

fewer guns boomed, for lack of targets at which to shoot. The shouting died, and order came out of the battle's chaos.

Troopers who had been left up on the ridge to guard overcoats and haversacks left behind by their comrades when they charged at dawn now came down the slope to say they had been attacked by Indians and that Custer's staghound Blucher had been killed.

From the wagon train that had just arrived in the village, it was now possible for the troopers to resupply themselves with ammunition, badly depleted during the attack. They began firing again, without much success but with great enthusiasm, at the mounted Indians on top of the cliff.

Lieutenant Godfrey of Troop K returned with the herd of Indian ponies, numbering close to a thousand, and stationed men on all sides of them to keep them in place. He rode to Custer and saluted him. "General, beyond those bluffs where the mounted warriors are, there are a number of other villages not visible from here. And I heard firing on the far side of the river that may have been Major Elliott and his men. He could be in trouble, sir."

Custer's face for the first time showed concern, but not for Elliott. "How many villages, Lieutenant? How many lodges in all?"

Godfrey frowned. "I can't say, General, because I didn't go far enough. But I must have seen a couple of hundred or more tipis, and I'm sure I didn't see anywhere near all of them."

By now, the number of mounted Indians on the bluff downstream had increased. Custer thought there must have been two or three hundred at least and more kept coming all the time. Godfrey saluted and returned to his troop, his face showing his own concern, not for the Indian villages hidden by the bluff but for Major Elliott and his nineteen men.

He made sure the Indian pony herd was secure, and stationed enough troopers on the uphill side of it to guard against any Indian attempt to repossess it. When he returned to the valley floor, Custer ordered him to supervise the burning of the huge pile of Indian lodges and household goods.

Still worried about Elliott, Godfrey obeyed. Slowly the pile caught fire, and as the fire spread, the column of black smoke rose higher and higher into the air.

Despite the fire's crackling, Godfrey still thought he could occasionally hear the sound of firing downstream in the direction Elliott and his men had gone. Once more he went to Custer and saluted. "General, I think I still can hear firing downstream beyond those bluffs in the direction Major Elliott took his men. Don't you think, sir, that we could send a couple of troops to see?"

Custer slowly shook his head. "I hardly think it was firing you heard, Lieutenant. Captain Myers has been fighting down there all morning and if there had been any firing, I am sure he would have reported it."

Reluctantly, Godfrey retired. By now, the mounted braves on the bluff were approaching, obviously enraged by the burning of the tipis. Two troops were formed between the river and the bluff and the order was given to charge. They did, for a short distance, and the Indians retired out of range.

Custer dismounted from his horse, sat on a rock, and considered the situation. He had within his grasp the victory he had been looking for. He had destroyed one large village, that of Black Kettle, the most influential of the Cheyenne chiefs. The dead count among the Indians was a hundred and three men. For political reasons no count had been made of the women and children killed. Fifty-three squaws and children were prisoners, among them the beautiful girl Custer had noticed earlier.

Custer's own casualties were few. Captain Hamilton and one enlisted man were the only ones killed. Fourteen officers and men had been wounded, only one, Captain Barnitz, seriously.

Elliott and his nineteen men were missing, but Custer hoped they were all right and could fight their way out of whatever they had gotten themselves into. They were downstream behind a bluff surrounded by hundreds of armed, angry Indians. If they had run into serious trouble, there was little chance they were still alive, even less they would be alive by the time a rescue party, if one were sent, could get to them.

Besides that, to commit a rescue party large enough to engage all the hostiles downstream from here, several hundred of whom were visible on the bluff, would be to jeopardize that which was already in his grasp. Victory. Glory. Vindication.

Elliott had been a fool. His melodramatic words upon leaving had proved him to be a fool. Custer had no intention of jeopardizing this overwhelming victory by committing a large part of his force to trying to rescue men already presumed dead.

It was nearing noon. The pyre of the lodges and the Indians' household goods and food supplies was now shooting flames fifty feet into the air. The black column of smoke must have towered a thousand feet, and was drifting toward the southeast on the prevailing breeze.

Among the orders given him by General Sheridan at Camp Supply was one that he destroy the Indians' pony herd. He therefore issued orders that several cases of ammunition be brought, along with several new Spencer carbines from the supply wagon carrying ordnance. He found himself a spot near the pony herd, where the bulk of the herd would protect the trooper guards on the other side of it from his bullets. He then methodically began firing, and at each shot, an Indian pony dropped, some to lie kicking briefly, but most lying still as soon as they struck the ground.

The other horses began galloping, milling around in a circle, which gave Custer moving targets, more to his liking. The Indians on the top of the bluff once more started down, obviously outraged over the slaughter, but they were turned back by two troops dispatched for that purpose.

Their turning back in no way implied cowardice on the part of the Cheyennes. It simply meant they recognized the superiority of the seven-shot Spencers over their own bows and arrows, which were inaccurate even at short range, and their old muzzle-loaders

183

which, once fired, were useless for several minutes while being reloaded for firing again.

Custer continued to slaughter horses, apparently having an insatiable appetite for it. In truth, he was preparing in his mind his report to Sheridan and to any possible board of inquiry that later might be convened.

His failure to dispatch a rescue party after Elliott was certain to come under extreme criticism, but he would say he had sent several scouting parties out in an attempt to ascertain Elliott's whereabouts. Otherwise, his losses had been negligible.

It was the victory he had wanted so desperately, needed so desperately, to restore his tarnished reputation with his superiors. He would not jeopardize it now by pursuing it further. God only knew how many Indians waited beyond that bluff. Enough to annihilate his command, perhaps. Enough to administer a defeat that would take the place of the victory now in his hands. As for Elliott, he had been a melodramatic fool. He had shouted for a brevet or a coffin, and a coffin was what he was going to get. Custer didn't even feel any real regret, either for Elliott or for the nineteen men who had ridden so recklessly away with him. They were dead. There had been no firing from down-river for some time now.

So he continued shooting horses, heating the barrel of each rifle until it was too hot to hold, then discarding it for another one. Eventually he tired of this sport, turned the completion of the slaughter over to several enlisted men, and left.

Weary and satiated, he returned to his horse and gave orders to prepare to retire from the field. In his mind, he totaled up his victory. Fifty-one Indian lodges had been destroyed. A hundred and three Indian men were dead, their bodies counted and rechecked. Over fifty women and children had been taken prisoner. The pony herd destroyed.

It had been a long, long day, but somehow it seemed to have passed very quickly indeed. Now the sun was down and dusk was settling across the land.

Custer thought of the hundreds of mounted, armed Cheyennes downstream behind that buff. He issued orders that the command would move out immediately, citing when questioned by one or two of his officers his worry about the safety of his huge supply train toiling southward through the snow some twenty or thirty miles away.

Leaving the burned lodges, the sprawled bodies, the eight to nine hundred dead or dying Indian ponies, the command finally, as the moon rose, made its way up out of the valley of the Washita with the band blaring "Ain't I Glad to Get Out of the Wilderness." Only when they had reached what Custer considered to be a safe distance did they halt to rest.

Custer's claim of concern for his supply train was belied by the halt. The truth was that he now was on high ground and felt himself able to repulse any attack that might be made. Besides, he knew that Indians seldom fight at night.

CHAPTER
TWENTY-ONE

Clay Holley was no more than a dozen yards behind Major Elliott as he galloped away in pursuit of the handful of escaping Cheyennes. He caught up in a matter of minutes. He heard no roar from Custer ordering the major to return, and he doubted if Elliott would have returned even had he been ordered to.

Elliott was extremely young to hold the rank of major. His face was boyish and in some ways immature. Holley would have guessed he was a lieutenant had it not been for the major's insignia he wore.

The other eighteen men strung out for fifty yards behind. There were large trees here and underbrush, but the Indians had been in this spot long enough to wear paths through the underbrush so that it was not impossible to penetrate.

The women and children the retreating braves had originally been trying to protect had now scattered and disappeared into the underbrush. But the warriors remained in a body, running swiftly and silently, keeping their distance ahead of Elliott and his mounted troopers because it was easier for them to get through the narrow paths in the heavy brush.

186

Holley's eyes were still on that white cloth waving like a flag, and the warriors they were pursuing reminded him of the coyotes around his ranch. They would come in close, yapping and taunting the ranch dogs until finally the dogs would be unable to stand it any more. The dogs would set out in pursuit, with the coyotes easily staying just ahead of them.

Holley had lost more than one dog that way. Over the nearest ridge, or in some nearby gully, the coyotes would turn and literally tear the dog apart. This chase of these retreating Cheyennes reminded him of that, and he wondered if total destruction was what the retreating Cheyenne warriors had in mind for them. Probably it was.

They burst out of the trees. The warriors they were pursuing had disappeared into a village of closely set tipis, still a couple of hundred yards short of the fluttering piece of cloth.

They reappeared on the far side of the small cluster of tipis, mounted now. Turning on their horses' backs, they fired at Elliott and his pursuing troopers, made obscene gestures, and shouted taunts.

Nothing could have been more skillfully designed to infuriate the major, who had received like treatment from the Indians around Fort Dodge all summer long. Waving his saber, the major roared, "Let's get 'em, men!"

Beyond, at a point half a mile or so below the village Custer had destroyed, the river took a bend to the left and here, instead of a gradual slope rising to the crest of the ridge, the terrain became steeper, the slope ending in a rocky rim twenty-five feet high that guarded a bluff on which now were appearing more mounted Cheyennes.

Visible beyond the river bend, villages stretched out almost as far as the eye could see. And in all these villages, Indians scurried around like ants. Warriors emerged from them, mounted, dressed, armed, and ready to do battle with the whites.

Clay Holley glanced at Major Elliott's face. It showed no dismay at the number of hostiles facing him. Instead it glowed with the same excitement it had shown earlier. Elliott, in common with most frontier commanders, thought a handful of well-mounted, well-equipped U. S. Army troopers could whip all the hostiles on the plains.

He had seen the decisive way Custer had annihilated the village of Black Kettle. Apparently he thought he could do the same with those facing him.

Now the fluttering piece of petticoat was only a hundred and fifty yards ahead. And just beyond the Cheyennes were firming up, still milling, but gathering numbers with every passing moment.

Holley hipped around in his saddle. He had already pointed out the fluttering piece of petticoat to those who had promised to help him, but now he pointed it out again.

Denton bawled, "Now?"

Holley shook his head. He wanted to be still closer. He wanted Elliott and the others to be engaged with the Cheyennes. He knew then he would have the better chance to save the life of Julia and Sally and her boy.

188

By now all sound had faded from behind. The wind, a crosswind, had carried away the sounds of firing by Custer's men.

If the men with Elliott felt any doubt, they didn't show it. They were caught up in the excitement of battle, in the glorious galloping movement of their horses, in the consciousness of the powerful Spencer carbines in their hands. They were infected with Elliott's enthusiasm and recklessness. And they had one other thing to keep them from having doubts. They knew that behind them was Custer, with seven hundred well-armed men, who, if they got into trouble, would certainly come to their aid.

Nearly abreast of the tipi with that fluttering scrap of petticoat, Holley spurred his horse savagely until the animal came abreast of Major Elliott. He didn't want this little group of men, who he believed were doomed, to think he was deserting them. He bawled, "Major!"

Elliott turned his head, his glance questioning.

Holley shouted, pointing to the piece of petticoat, "Looks like some kind of signal, sir. Maybe white captives there. Permission to check it out?"

Elliott hesitated only momentarily. Then he bawled, "All right, private! Take a couple of men! When Custer comes, tell him where we've gone!"

For an instant, Holley was almost overcome with amazement that this boyish major with so much courage and so little judgment would even let him go. He was more amazed that Elliott expected Custer to come to his aid.

He yelled, "Sir!" giving Elliott a quick salute. Elliott seemed to forget him almost immediately. Holley glanced around at Denton, Hines, and Daniels. They had seen him talking with Elliott and, while they could not have heard the words the two had exchanged, they could not have missed the substance. Holley waved an arm toward the tipi with the petticoat fluttering over it and veered his horse aside, spurring him hard, forcing him to maintain a steady gallop toward it.

He knew well that if the other squaws inside that tipi saw U. S. Army troopers galloping toward the particular tipi, they would know their purpose was the rescue of the white squaws they disliked anyway. Holley would arrive to find Julia and Sally dead. His only chance, therefore, lay in reaching the tipi before he was seen by those inside.

Glancing back, he saw Elliott and his remaining fifteen troopers still galloping toward the growing concentration of warriors down the Washita. He felt a touch of sadness and regret because he knew all sixteen men were doomed.

Maybe he and the three with him were also doomed. But their chances of survival were vastly increased by the fact that Elliott and his remaining troopers had captured and held the attention of the hostiles ahead of them.

Now the tipi with the fluttering piece of petticoat was only a few yards ahead. Suddenly Frank Denton hauled his horse to an abrupt halt. On the ground where he had halted was a child, a three-year-old, dressed in buckskins like the Indians. But his hair was light and short. He was dead. His belly had been ripped open with a knife and his entrails lay spread out upon the ground.

Even more than before, Holley knew how urgent was the rescue of Julia and Sally Denton. In blind retribution for Custer's attack, someone, probably a squaw, had ripped young Frankie open, killing him instantly. The same might happen to Julia, or to Sally, or to both of them if they were not rescued immediately.

Denton dismounted and gathered the pitiful remains into his arms. He remounted his horse, but Holley, glancing back, knew he was no longer useful as a fighting man. He would probably get himself killed too, as preoccupied as he was with his grief.

But Clay Holley had no time to worry about that. With his arm, he gestured forward toward the tipi with the fluttering petticoat at the top of the smoke-flap pole. The three galloped to the entrance. Holley was down and running before his horse had a chance to halt. He burst through the flap, carbine in his hands.

Julia stood facing two Cheyenne squaws, a gleaming knife in her hand. Instantly Holley's eyes took in the bulge at her middle and he knew she still had her child.

The other two women in the tipi, the squaws, also had knives, and were approaching Julia from different directions. The outcome was predictable.

Clay Holley, with his wife for the first time so close, so near, did not hesitate. He fired, and one of the squaws slumped to the ground. Clay swung his gun toward the other one.

This one apparently valued her life more than she cherished her hatred of her buck's white squaw. She threw down the knife and held her arms out away from her body.

Julia, dropping the knife, ran to her husband's arms. He held her close to him, but briefly, for there was no time now for this. He said, "Come on. Where's Sally?"

"Dead. She killed herself."

"Come on, then. Frankie's dead too. Killed after Custer began his attack."

The pair fled from the tipi, and just outside Holley boosted Julia to the back of his horse. He well knew that the violent movement of a galloping or running horse might cause her to lose her child, but immediate escape was an absolute necessity.

He glanced around for Denton, saw him sitting his horse less than fifty feet away still holding the mutilated body of young Frankie in his arms.

To Hines he bawled, "Get the reins of his horse and drag him along with us!"

Hines complied. They could now hear, from farther downstream, the firing of Elliott's Spencers, the firing too of the Indians' ancient old smoothbores, which had a deep-throated roar the Spencers did not possess.

For only an instant did Holley hesitate about the direction he would take. To go help Elliott, who had so generously released him, would be to put Julia and their child in deadly jeopardy, perhaps ensure their deaths.

To return to Custer would probably subject him and those with him to court-martial because Custer would be anxious to find a scapegoat for his own failure to send a rescue party after Elliott.

His own conscience was clear. He had not deserted Elliott. He had obtained permission from the major to leave and check out any possible white captives in the lodge.

Only one course remained. He must now get away, as quickly as possible, both from the Indians and from the cavalry that had assaulted them.

North, then, he rode, with his three companions behind him, with Denton seeming numb with the tiny, disemboweled body of Frankie Denton in his arms. Finally, clear of the valley and the Indian villages it contained, Holley stopped. He said, "Frank, put him down. He's dead and there's nothing you can do for him."

Hines dismounted and to the still-stunned Denton said, "Let me have him, Frank."

Numbly, Frank Denton surrendered the mutilated body of his nephew. Hines laid him on the ground and covered him with his own blanket. Then, with the faint popping of rifle fire still behind them, the five rode north.

Holley thought that Custer had his victory. Regrettably, Elliott, whom he had liked, would get his coffin instead of his brevet. But most important from his own point of view, he had Julia, warm and safe, in the saddle in front of him. With luck, she still would have their child. With luck, they could pick up their lives where they had been broken off.

Behind them the din of battle faded. And at last they were riding alone across the vast and empty plain.

The look that was in Julia's eyes whenever she turned and looked at him made him feel about ten feet tall. He held her gently, and he slowed his horse to a smooth walk because he knew her time was near.

CHAPTER
TWENTY-TWO

Custer's report to Sheridan, of which he made a rough draft at their first night's halt, reported among other things that scouting parties sent out to find Major Elliott had returned, reporting no trace of him. In truth these scouting parties were so small they feared to venture too far from the main command for fear of being cut off from it and killed, the way they believed Elliott had been.

In order to give credence to his claim, later made, that he feared for the safety of the large, unwieldy wagon train, he sent Captain West with his squadron to locate the wagon train and protect it from possible attack.

Custer had the captives brought to his tent. Among them, he again saw the beautiful young squaw whose name, he was told through one of the Osage interpreters, was Monahsetah. When the others were taken away, she remained behind.

Troopers slept as though they were dead, but Custer himself was buoyed by excitement still, and his head was filled with thoughts of the reception his spectacular victory would receive. He had the energy for

195

Monahsetah, and he still had the energy to arise at daybreak, the hour he had ordered reveille.

Haggard, red-eyed troopers readied themselves and their mounts for another long day's march. More than a few of them were puzzled over this precipitous retreat. They had destroyed the village of Black Kettle. Their losses had been negligible. They could have pursued the victory and destroyed the Cheyennes' fighting capability for good.

Instead they were retreating at a pace that almost amounted to a rout. Finally, in the afternoon, a long-delayed bivouac was made. In timber on the rim of the Washita Basin, a position Custer considered highly defensible, he ordered a halt to rest the men and horses and to permit them to prepare a meal of hot food. They had made contact at ten that morning with Captain West and the huge wagon train, and ever since it had toiled along in their wake.

Hay and grain were now available for the used-up horses. Food in plentiful quantity was available for the men. Fires were built and the smell of cooking food filled the air. Several deer had been killed and brought in by the Osages, and the savory odor of cooking fresh meat helped lift the spirits of the men.

Custer had his tent set up, along with his folding writing desk and chair. And now he wrote his dispatch to Sheridan. When it was completed, he called for a courier and sent him on his way, accompanied by an appropriate escort, to Sheridan. And then Custer slept, with Monahsetah at his side.

196

Dawn saw the regiment on the march again, toiling north through the melting snow, following the trail they had made earlier coming south. A day's march out of Camp Supply, Custer sent another dispatch to General Sheridan, advising him that the regiment would arrive at a certain hour tomorrow and would pass in review for the general's approval.

At the appointed hour on December 2, the long, "victorious" column marched down the slope into the valley where stood Camp Supply to pass in review before Sheridan and his staff. The band blared "Garry Owen," over and over again. Troops of the 19th Kansas and the 3rd Infantry, garrisoned at Camp Supply, cheered as Custer, accompanied by his white scouts and Osage trackers and followed by the group of captured women and children on foot, marched before the squat, blocky Sheridan. Custer, his long hair tumbling over the shoulders of his buckskin jacket, flashed his saber in salute to his general.

Hamilton and the trooper were buried the following day. Some of the wounded troopers were returned to duty immediately. Others remained in the camp hospital until they could also be returned to duty.

Preparations were begun immediately to resume the campaign against the Cheyennes. This time the 19th Kansas would ride with the 7th Cavalry. Sheridan, personally in command of this column, would end the Indian problem once and for all by abolishing the Indian.

Custer, somewhat chastened, rode along as one of Sheridan's subordinates. Sheridan had not criticized him openly and had seemed satisfied, even pleased with the success Custer had had. But this campaign in itself, to Custer, implied that Sheridan was not altogether satisfied.

There were scouts by the dozen, both white and Indian. There was an Irishwoman to cook for Custer. There were two Cheyenne women to act as interpreters. And as usual there was a long supply train.

With the supply train rode Daniel Brewster, who was seeking his sister, captured by the Cheyennes the previous summer at about the same time Julia Holley was taken from her home. Also sought was another prisoner, Sarah Smith.

Their route pointed toward a location south of the Washita "battlefield." But when they reached a plateau eight miles or so downstream from it, Sheridan and Custer took an escort and rode north to view the scene of the "victory" and if possible to ascertain the fate of Elliott and his nineteen men.

A stench lay over the area, helped little by the cold, frosty air that lay unmoving in the valley. Crows and vultures rose screaming and flapping from the corpses of both humans and horses. Wolves slunk away, teeth bared, and a few abandoned dogs still lingered in the valley.

Custer led Sheridan to a ridge where he explained how the battle had taken place. Then, with a correspondent from the New York *Herald* and a small escort, they followed the south bank of the Washita in the direction Elliott and his men had gone.